MW01489437

Gatherings Volume XI

The En'owkin Journal of
First North American Peoples

Flight Scape:
a multi-directional collection
of Indigenous creative works

Fall 2000

edited by Florene Belmore

Theytus Books Ltd.
Penticton, BC

Gatherings
The En'owkin Journal of First North American Peoples
Volume XI   2000

Canadian Cataloguing in Publication Data
Main entry under title:

Gatherings

Annual.
ISSN 1180-0666   ISBN 0-919441-93-9

1. Canadian literature (English)--Indian authors--Periodicals.* 2.
Canadian literature (English)--20th century--Periodicals.* 3
American literature--Indian authors--Periodicals. 4. American
literature--20th century--Periodicals. I. En'owkin International
School of Writing. II. En'owkin Centre.
PS8235.I6G35   C810.8'0897   CS91-031483-7
PR9194.5.I5G35

Editor: Florene Belmore
Cover Art: Margaret Orr
Design & Layout: Florene Belmore

Please send submissions and letters to *Gatherings*, En'owkin
Centre, R.R.2, Site 50, Comp. 8, Penticton, BC, V2A 6J7, Canada
Previously published works are not considered.

*The publisher acknowledges the support of the Canada Council,
Department of Canadian Heritage and the British Columbia Arts
Council in the publication of this book.*

Table of Contents

Table of Contents

Table of Contents

Editor's Note

After celebrating ten years of Gatherings last year, it is an honour and a pleasure to edit the first volume of the second decade of *Gatherings: The En'owkin Journal of First North American Peoples*. As an Aboriginal publishing house dedicated to Aboriginal Literatures, Theytus Books is also proud to bring the publication of the only annual literary journal for Aboriginal voices into a new era. In this eleventh volume, we have sought submissions under the theme "Flight Scape: A multi-directional collection of Indigenous creative works."

In the past year, I have played a lead role in developing the theme, soliciting submissions, reading through the submissions, making the selections, going through the editorial process with the authors, and compiling and producing the Journal. As usual, many other people have also committed their time and talent toward the effort required to publish this journal each year. I'd like to thank Rasunah Marsden for her valuable imput. And of course the staff of the En'owkin Centre, a special thanks to Regina Gabriel. Many thanks also to the Aboriginal authors for having the courage to write and the generosity to share their work. You inspire us all.

I now realize what a monumental task it is for the editors and Theytus Books to publish Gatherings on an annual basis. However, I also understand the importance of publishing a current and vibrant collection of Aboriginal Literatures each year. It is, in a sense, a documentation of our voice that affirms our continuing presence both on the landscape and in the literary world. Aboriginal authors continue to persevere, drawing back on our ancestors and traditions to find a solid foundation, and reaching out into uncharted territory to develop new literary techniques.

Florene Belmore

Blueberries

The end of summer
and we pick blue
berries, pluck them
with delicate precision,
open ourselves to the goodness
that is theirs
drop the offering
onto our ready tongue
and drift into heavy clouds
bringing us to remember

friends who move
marry
make pies and jam
they ate as children for their own children,
holding to the sweetness
they once loved.

and divorced
that's them too
when fingers cramp, stop,
mouths close in denial,
and the heart's want
is replaced by the sickly feeling
of having too much
too little.

But here kneeling in the ruins
of stumps as far as the eye can see,
we take these berries
blue as the new life they are,
        in gratitude

humility,
yet lustful for the taking.
The dusty logging road at our backs
we stand, stretch to leave
at day's end
and laugh in our full desire
all the way home.

Detour

Once upon a time I rode shotgun for a trickster kind of guy who thought we lived in a western, and it would always stay that way. The Lone Ranger and Tonto riding into the sunset. Both of us wanting to be the Lone Ranger. That's us in the picture he carried around in his head, six years old, leather holsters and cowboy hats. Fringed shirts and moccasins from my auntie. The two of us, into the world the same time, the same neighbourhood, and before long crawling into cars through windows, wrecks with doors wired shut, locked in as we had been from birth. Roaring down the road in one gear. Full speed come what may.

I wonder
where you are these days
last time
you were working in a distillery
and bought an empty barrel
you soaked
and let sit
later
we drank the whiskey water
and got piss drunk
for old time's sake
talk about a hangover

How many times did we make it into town and finish up at the Sportsman's Hotel on some Friday evening. Meeting the folks from up and down the line who would come in and get loosened up. Until we too got bent out of shape and then back into the car and back into the bush. Thought we could live like that forever. Though I remember once looking around at all the boozed up old timers and swearing their end wouldn't be mine. Some weren't even old. Like Terry. When the doctors opened him up to stop the hemorrhaging, they took one look and closed him back up again. His stomach looked like a tire blown to hell from all the Aqua Velva and cleaning fluid.

Last time we rode together
you ended up with a woman
you picked up
hitchhiking
you always
had a way with women
about the time
I decided
enough was enough
it was time
to move on
about the time
you lost your son

Remember? We weren't much older than him when got stuck between those two fence posts. We'd been out raiding gardens for strawberries, your own mother's, which always seemed so absurd because she gave us all we wanted, but I guess you preferred to eat them at night with the earth still clinging. Or was it sitting in front of her with a blank face when she complained about the little devils. We were heading down the lane when a car appeared, and we dashed for a gateway and got jammed together. Like so much that came later, we had to wiggle our way out of that one. Like the time you ran away from home because you had fallen in lust with a girl up the line and were bound to get to her. And me walking the tracks behind you wishing I were fishing. Why I tagged along, I still don't know. Though I suppose for the ride. Always the ride, and a wild one it was, riding high in trickster style.

Prayer

I placed a braid of sweetgrass
on your coffin and sat quietly.
Outside the sky was dark,
and I wore dark glasses
because it was still too bright.

At the graveyard the priest blessed
your passing. An Anishinaabe Elder
appeared, laid down tobacco
and spoke in your language.
Someone asked me who he was
and I answered a part of your life
beyond ours.

You said you wanted a feast
for all your family and friends.
My heart split, I dug my fork
deep into it and chewed
and chewed unable to let go.
The old people held my hand
and told me stories about you
as I prayed for rain.

Unless serious action is taken few Indigenous languages to Canada will survive in the 21st century. The Royal Commission on Aboriginal Peoples

Now that the Galleons have Landed

Where are the words
of Turtle Island?
rooted in earth
painted on stone
and bark,
carved
into cedar
totems,
a thousand year old
memory

What is left
but dream
new words
written on paper
in the smoke
prayer
in the angry
loss
in the weak
catch
emptied
and flailing.

What is left
but to struggle
with mouth
hooked
and discover
this tongue

fitted perfectly
is the sound
of a prisoner
on a boat
bound
to wailing
death

For the ancestors
huddled before
the story of fire,
Nanabush
his laughter
spilling
like his seed
blooming
into the *tikinagan*,   (cradleboard)
a baby
who sings
every syllable
of her mother
earth

This loss
my burden
as I gasp
to stay the course
in this language
shoved into
my relations
and now gathered
in my own
bundle
in my own
voice
to deafen me.

Burial Dress

Carefully		Prayerfully
Inside, outside		Sinew sewn
Our Ways	of	Old Days
Ash and Fire		Spirit home

Elk skin		Doe skin
Supple, softened		Forest grown
Breath dress		Death dress
Shell and Bead		Woman's own

Fingering		Fringing
Back, forth		Together alone
Gentle sway	of	Whitened frays
Platform and Pyre		Indian bones

Lost and Found In My Own Life

The questions always came, pouring down in rain
or whooshing past me in wind. It was easier to avoid
them on perfect blue days, on brilliant sunlit mornings.

But sooner or later the clouds pressed me for answers
and I'd retreat into darkness. I had no one to ask
in whitened kitchens or on wooden Roman pews.

I learned to accept the void, turn my eyes inward,
travel without a guide. Oh, there were always stories
told over some holiday glass, but nothing served serious;

merely wild imaginings of relatives, daft with aged
mentality, dismissed in unproved authority. Yet my spirit
housed a fire of voices pleading through the storm.

The answers began without warning in my forty-third year.
A slow rain of knowing started. Soon I was riding the river
of my own history and ready to meet streams of those before.

Hence—hidden voices cleared the curtain of the wind
to reveal sacred word and thought. By flaming night
I heard them calling me by a new and familiar name.

I saw faces peering through the gauze of rain,
jowled woman faces laid precisely over my
grandmother's face, my mother's face and mine.

I recognized myself at last.
The questions still come. But these days
I know where to turn for the answers.
I know where to turn.

Fancy Dancer

My men have no hold on me
they are dreams I left behind
they are memories I forget most times
no more tears for me

then

you dance, jump into the sky and bend your leg coming down,
six feet high and sweaty glistening movement you are free you
are the softness in my knees your breath I feel as it leaves your
lips and as you dance closer to me my body moves and I am
dancing too and you spin and spin away from me leaving only
that sexy smile to show you saw

the song ends
cuz all songs end
and I quickly turn away—
no more tears for me

Love Story

She met him on the ball field
Strong, tall and straight
He threw
She caught
They knew

And then they moved
Onto parties and dances
Playing pool
Friends always around
And when they weren't
Just the stars
And they knew

The first time wasn't so bad
A push
But she held him
And calmed him
And loved him even more

Sometimes she'd complain
To him, to friends
She'd say I'll leave
I'll take the kids
I'll go far away
And he'd say
I'm sorry I love you
And cry

If you lived there
Maybe you know
How the next part goes
How she falls

Out of herself
How she bruises
In secret places
How she learns
A careful walk

Such an old story
Played out so well
It was the only one they knew.

The Right Thing

Good God its horrid
and bad
just plain sucks
for *them*
she says
rolling her eyes
and squeezing her face
together—so narrow and tight
skinny slim and white white.
She says
I want to work in human rights
right what's wrong
make things right.
Right.

I watch her make bread
kneading the dough
bony fists moving on it hard
pushing it down
pulling it up
fitting it into the pan.
Racism, sexism, ageism
homophobia
she spits them out like fire.
This same heat
I can feel
upon my face
when she laughs
at my ignorance.

Later her hand upon my shoulder
tell me about your people
she says

Dawn Dumont

I talk openly
freeing my stories
they enter the air
round faces
and dimpled smiles
bubbling laughter
at unkind times.
Shaking her head,
she says
how awful
I am going to change things.
I am going to make them better.
I am going to make them right.
Right.

Untitled

Anishinaabe
he says and smiles
and I smile back
we have a secret
just me and him
on this corner
he begs
got a styrofoam cup of coins
but he starts Monday he says
got a job just today
where you from, we ask
that telling detail
he says poormans
and I know where
that is
ka-wa-ca-toose
I say-he nods
his mother once told him the name
we're far from home
the green prairies
the land of skies
the patient wind
the biting cold
but it seems warmer than here
why'd you leave
I think
but I know
his answer is too much like my own
to really want to hear
dreams are bigger than small reserves
and we leave to try them all
and sometimes—
we end up street corners
cold alone and far from home

Message from the Conqueror

At first I conquer you, how does not really matter. I could beat you into the ground, or persuade you to accept my beliefs and values, thus casting aside all that makes you different from me —there are many other ways. Then I take what I need and want whether it is important to you or not, whether it defines your people or not. I do not care. I see only my children, my possessions and my dreams. I cannot see your dreams. I cannot see who you are. Your children, I see, but they just seem dirty to me. When you argue that I have done you wrong, I cannot agree. To me and my kind, it was sympathetic, not cruel. And if cruel, then certainly necessary. True, in my movies I admit you had an Eden but in my courts you were just as mean as me. I did what I did to survive. You argue, you plead, you cry, you throw your hands to the sky—sometimes, in despair, you die. All of that is rather sad. I do sympathize. But when your offer your hand and ask for help—I do not want to respond. With your begging eyes and hopeful smile, I want to cast you down. I want to pretend there is no you, or if there is, then only the clean and whitewashed will I recognize. I do not want to play anymore. I want you just to go away. I do not want to hear your past, that you were victimized—I will not listen to these lies. Let me be. I have things to do. Get on with it—my world has no place for you.

Banana-Rama-Shama
(or, Political Bananas)

(Yes, we have no bananas,
We have no bananas today!)

1

They always come in *unreal yellow*
Like the unbruised skin of a
Chinese Courtesan in comic books.
Each one is a structural marvel,
A work of architectural perfection,
As if designed by the pioneering genius
of a corps of American engineers.
They seem so polished,
Though they are not stones,
And rarely, if at all,
They exhibit a brown spot
Fading into appearance,
A blemish of mortality,
Not an unsightly liver-spot or cancerous mole,
But the barest wisp of freckle, lightly dusted,
And tinged with the eclipsed penumbra of dusky-red.

2

Their sweetness is a disgusting sham,
A sugary ruse,
For they conceal
Within their pre-wrapped goodness
The green bitterness of poverty,
The bloated bellies of infants,
The bloody suppression of peasants
And the slaughter of justice, of morality, of innocence . . .
All that dearth and death!
In thickly thrusting groves

Which bristle like a bunch of green-gloved fists
Clenched as if to crush the latest Revolutionary Party,
They appear like a judgment
Over this fertile land parcelled out
To the Banana Barons who hold a monopoly
On this Bonanza of Bananas.

3

They conceal more than we will ever know,
Like the pungent spice of death
Bereft of its keening odour and taste.
I love to eat them,
To slowly peel their
Sun-warmed halcyon ripeness
Like soft horns of carved ivory.
I crave to touch them while
They lie mounded in tempting heaps in green bins
Like furless and plump golden-yellow bats,
And sleeping like quiescent pods in supermarkets . . .
Then, when nobody is looking, I deftly
Lick the invisible film of ecstasy
Which sticks to the tips of my
Guilty fingers.
I cannot help myself.
No.

4

I like my bananas doused in milk and sugar.
I like them sliced on my morning cereal,
Like mushy coins of fibrous fruit.
I bought them at *39 cents* **per pound**
At the local Safeway Store.
To whom do I pay for my breakfast,
To whom do I owe an outstanding account?
8 cents **to the Safeway store;**
12 cents **to the transporters and distributors;**

15 cents **to the Banana Barons**
Who make all this deliciousness possible;
3 cents for me **because of a store-sale;**
And *1 cent* **for the pickers and washers**
Who live in shanties like vagrants, beggars, and thieves.
Yes, the exploitation of poor workers is "good for the economy."

5
I burp.
I have a slight bit of indigestion.
Hopefully, tonight, I will be well enough
To sip my banana daiquiri
Topped off with a big slice of banana-cream pie.
I *live* for these small pleasures,
My petty addictions,
Which some have said have conquered
The lands and lives of less fortunate souls.
Yet I have earned the right to gorge myself,
The right to consume the plunder of the world,
An international cornucopia of
Red-orange mangos, kiwis, coconuts, and those ever-
succulent guavas!
If not me, then who else will profit by the losses of others?
So beautiful in their broad glossy leaves,
So abundant in their elongated, lobe-swollen, yellow
crescents,
They await to be plucked,
To be baptized in sparkling sheen of purifying acids,
And then trained and boated and trucked
To market.
Who will profit? I say.

6
Ecuador, Honduras, Guatemala . . .
Dole, Delmonte, Chicquita . . .
The game is the same,

Only the brand-names are different.
What matters to me how these
Long yellow loaves of honeyed manna come to
Cheer my table in the morning?
What care I for the lean brown bodies that
Waste in green-dripping heat,
So that I might savour
The Glut of Paradise
Like some Plantation-owner perspiring gently in white linen?
Can we love whom we are not?
Should we deny ourselves great plenitude
Because of the barren poverty and pain of another?
Should I blame myself
For my insatiable and rapacious desire
Which leads me to betray
The ban of boycotts
And to pursue the savagely selfish politics of consumption?
Left for two, maybe three days at most,
And already my bananas begin to rot
As if by some powerful inner corruption.

Fever

(an excerpt from "The Lake")

On the second day of the hunting trip, the *syilx* rounded a bend of the mountain. The land was still save for the chirr of grasshoppers jumping from the path of the nine horses and their riders. The heat was constant, but it was also light, a reminder of the height above the valley. Horse knew the country well, and rode easily, letting his horse follow the lead of the riders ahead.

Every so often Horse would turn to look behind. It was instinctual. He had to know the country they passed as well as the country they rode into. He also knew enough to watch for any signs of pursuit from either animals or from the Secwepmc, whose lands were very close.

Horse also had his mind elsewhere. Last night, just before setting up camp, Horse had watched as Coyote, *Sn-klip*, sat on a mound half a bowshot from the riders. *Sn-klip's* boldness, always there, was different this time. He ignored the other riders and stared at Horse, their eyes meeting and locking. "What are you trying to tell me?" Horse asked.

Sn-klip cocked his head to the left, his ears flapping forward.

Another rider, seeing this, grinned. "I think *Sn-klip* likes you."

Horse grinned back. "I guess he has good taste."

This set up a round of humour which lasted until the headman chose a camping site. By the time Horse looked around, *Sn-klip* had faded into the low underbrush, his lingering yip the only mark of his presence.

Sn-klip's bold stare was a message, this every *syilx* knew. The other riders also knew that the message was directed at Horse, and so left him to puzzle over what that message might be. The headman had spotted elk, and less than an hour's ride ahead.

Horse, being the last rider, paused at the bend. The steady low hoof beats of the horses ahead quickly became distant. Horse saw the distant blue ridges across the valley. Many days' ride away, some of the mountains glinted with streaks of white. Below where he sat the valley arced south, briefly hooked right and then faded straight south out of sight. The blue lake shimmered in the heat, its edges coloured a lighter blue where the water lapped ashore. The lake's surface was mottled with whitecaps, a contrast to the still warm air which hovered higher up the slopes.

Horse kept seeing *Sn-klip's* mocking gaze. Something warned him and he turned to look back where he had come from. The shock of seeing *Sn-klip* so close without any warning from his mount startled Horse. *Sn-klip* was again staring at Horse.

"What are you telling me, old one?"

Sn-klip was crouched on all fours, his head tilted forward and his long ears laid back in a posture Horse hadn't seen *Sn-klip* assume before.

At the moment their eyes met once again, a wind from the south brought a quick chill to the air. The tree branches all around remained still while the gusts of air made Horse's mount nervous. *Sn-klip* was gone once more by the time Horse had regained control of his mount. Horse suddenly felt the air and sun spin around him, and he held onto his mount's mane while the dizziness first swept over him, through him, and then was gone as quickly as the return of the still air.

* * * *

On the fifth day the hunters returned from a successful hunt. The camp knew long before their arrival of their coming, and the hunting party was met well before they came within sight of the twenty lodges. While most of the hunters were joyful in arriving, Horse was quiet. None of the other riders had felt the wind which blew through him, nor had the trees stirred. The headman told Horse he had had a vision, but couldn't explain Horse's being sick.

"What you have seen and felt you must bring to our Elders. They will know what signs to read."

Horse entered the teepee through the tulle mat cover. He accepted the fact that four Elders were waiting as though for him alone. He took a place near the fire, and thanked the Creator for his health and the health of the camp. Then he sat staring into the low flames until an Elder spoke from the opposite side of the fire.

"It was a good hunt."

Another Elder spoke. "The elk were large and swift, but not as swift as our young men."

"Yes, our young men can run fast."

The subdued laughter which followed trailed into the sounds of the firewood as it burnt, sending shadows jumping against the tulle mat walls. Although still daylight outside, it could have been any part of the day or night. Horse waited, his eyes glowing in the fire's light.

"How is old *Sn-klip*?"

Without looking away from the fire, Horse answered, "*Sn-klip* tried to tell me something."

"Only you?"

The voice, being low, could have come from any of the Elders.

"*Sn-klip* looked at me twice from close up."

"Aiyee. It is a sign, a dream."

"The second time there was a wind. It came and went without warning, and I felt sick. Like I was both warm and cold at the same time."

Another silence while someone threw another piece of wood into the flames.

"We must move camp soon. Some of the families will go root and berry gathering, while others will travel south. The fish are coming."

"The signs are good. It will be a good year for our people."

"*Sn-klip* talked with only Horse. Perhaps the message is only for him, not for our people."

"We should think on this. *Sn-klip's* boldness means something. I will talk to our shaman, the *tl'ekwelix*. When we gather again I will have some answers."

* * * *

The fire came on the wind, twists of flames spiralling north like the breath of a forest fire. Red tongues consumed everything in their way. The *syilx* fled in groups, scattering towards safety, but the flames increased, lifting people from their feet and sending them into the sky to disappear within the walls of fire. Other *syilx*, panicked beyond all reason, dove into the river, only to be swept away both by water and fire.

A black shape emerged from the sky. From its gaping mouth a tall woman strode towards Horse. She was one of them, a *syilx*, and yet so strange in her clothes of shimmering colours. She moved as the wind moved, a wave of motion and heat. Horse felt her coming like the coming of the first horse. The land shifted around the woman. Behind her loomed a floating object larger than the great peaks east of the valley.

The woman bore the carriage and marks of a warrior, a scar running down her left cheek.

"I welcome you to our land," Horse managed to greet the stranger.

The woman smiled and a warmth flooded through Horse which had nothing to do with the tongues of flame which continued to consume *syilx* everywhere.

"I have looked for you all my life," the woman bowed. "When I give to you, I give myself."

"Good words. How may I help you?"

"I am your future. The future of your people. You cannot help me. I come into your dreams, as I must."

"I understand. Can you help my people?"

The woman turned to gaze at the devastation. For a long time she stood motionless, the winds of flame brushing against her blue shimmering clothes without touching her, or scorching the cloth. She only turned back to Horse as the screams faded into the distance.

"Help isn't here. I cannot give you what you ask. But I am here as proof that we will continue."

Horse stared at the great object which hung in the sky. "Is there anything I can give you?"

The tall woman laughed. "Our people are dying around us, and you ask whether you can help me. No, you cannot help me. I bring you a simple message. The future will be yours when you own it."

The woman faded then, as she strode back into the floating object.

* * * *

"I cannot say what this dream means."

The *tl'ekwelix* nodded, his dark eyes unreadable as he leaned closer to the rocks and steam. The heat rolled around them, cleansing Horse's body but grating against something deep inside, a dark object which refused to move.

The *tl'ekwelix* turned at last to Horse. "I know this woman. She has appeared in my visions before, and in the visions of other Elders. We cannot say who she is. She has power, but that power cannot help us now. She is not from our times."

Horse waited, his body a river of sweat running down the black rock of his resistance. The *tl'ekwelix* threw another ladle of water onto the burning rocks, and a cloud of vapour obscured them from each other. When the vapour became heat and Horse could see the small wiry *tl'ekwelix*, the shaman was again looking towards him.

"We have been told of strange things coming our way. There are people whose skins are the colour of the clouds and more numerous than the grasshoppers along the hillsides. Our brothers down south tell of empty villages and bodies floating down rivers. Spirits roam this land now, angry spirits, strange spirits. In the last moon one of our villages has disappeared. The *syilx* who found the village felt sadness as he came close, but something held him back from going in the village. He saw an untended campfire in the middle of the village, but there were no *skahas*, no dogs anywhere. Just ghosts which pushed through the empty village. Not even the cry of babies. It was the strangest feeling of the *syilx's* life, and half of his head hair turned white from fear. He ran for two days, forgetting even his horse."

"*Aiyee*. Are we then to die without a fight?"

"We cannot fight ghosts, spirits. They are the land itself. They are the woman of your dreams, something not here. Something which we cannot touch."

* * * *

It came in the first cough. The young hunter had returned from a trip to a village southeast of the valley. Over the last day of travel he felt light-headed, and he moved as if he waded through water. A pleasant lethargy filled his body, and his hands turned red from warmth. By the time he reached his village, his hands contained a rash which he scratched, unable to help himself. He took to his tulle mats as soon as he arrived, and it was there that he coughed for the first time. His woman daubed his face as the fever took hold.

The *tl'ekwelix* whom she brought in to look at her man used bitterroot medicine to soak the young man's body. When the fever raged on, and red spots which turned into pustules began to dot the man's face, the *tl'ekwelix* tried to get the *syilx* to drink a bitter tea, but the fever and cough continued.

On the third day the *tl'ekwelix* was exhausted, and the woman was near hysterics, her weeping filling the teepee and the surrounding area, where a good number of *syilx* hovered, both in support for the young couple, and puzzled by the young man's fever and outbreaks, none of which anyone had seen in their lives.

The death rattle came when the *tl'ekwelix* left the teepee for more medicine, leaving the feverish man and his exhausted woman alone. She was sleeping but the *tl'ekwelix's* motions as he left stirred her from her sleep gradually. A strange sound woke her, a sound which sent chills through her skin. In the low firelight she could barely see her man wrapped in blankets. The moan came from the wind, or so she thought at first. But the rattle from across the fire, and the way her man's body seemed to heave into an impossible arc, made the young woman sit up. Fearful as she was of the figure which seemed to bend almost in half, the woman overcame her fear and screamed for help as she scrambled towards her man.

She heard an awful pop as though he had broken his back, and then, as others raced into the teepee, they watched as his throat rattled in a gurgle. It was like watching a twig unbend. As he breathed out, his body slowly flattened until he was once more stretched out on the mat.

The gathering of family and friends was enlarged by those who had heard of the man's strange death, and had come to support the village in its grief.

* * * *

Horse rode down the gentle slope towards the village. He had followed the *tl'ekwelix's* words, and spent the last twelve suns alone beneath a waterfall where he regularly bathed between sweats He was eager to be with his family.

The strange woman had appeared to him the previous night and urged him in soft tones to return home.

Horse's mind was on the woman of his dreams and he almost didn't notice the body in the stream until his mount shied away from the water. Startled, Horse left the woman's words to find himself staring at the body which lay face down in the stream, its arms and legs moving as though the boy were swimming. Horse didn't immediately do anything, respectively waiting for the boy to stand up or to move.

When neither happened, Horse felt the hair on his arms raise up in the warm air. Smoke spiralled up through the trees. Horse knew something was not right, and five minutes later he rode into camp. The first thing he noticed in the distance were the blankets, They were strewn throughout the camp and among the pine trees along the ridge. Horse dismounted and let his cayuse go. A cool breeze stirred the leaves, some of which fell into the smoldering ashes to create small bonfires which briefly flamed and then subsided. Horse limped to the nearest pile of blankets, and noticed the acrid smell of death as he drew closer. Beneath the blankets lay Wolverine, his eyes endlessly staring into the overcast sky. His face was ravaged by marks which Horse had heard the fur traders call small-pox.

Horse felt his feet leave the ground, floating as though afraid to touch Toom-Tem, Mother Earth. He forced himself to gather some foliage. Leaning over Wolverine, he closed the mystic's sightless eyes, letting go of his own grief with the song which took Wolverine into the world where Coyote waited for his children. East of the camp the river flowed over more bodies, also naked as women, children, old men and warriors had stripped their clothes off in a final frenzy to cool the bonfires which burned their souls crisp.

Time changes everything but memories, and the leaving of the Canada Geese, the falling of the leaves will be with the Okanagans forever.

Belinda The Biker

Belinda The Biker lived next door.
When she moved in, it was the third world war.

Her stereo blasted, shaking the walls.
The smell of leather hung in the halls.

People visited all through the night.
Very little movement in broad daylight.

The landlord was summoned early one morning.
"Too much noise; this is your warning!"

Doors were slammed, walls were knocked.
Down to the floor crashed my good wall clock.

"You have to pay!"
The landlord did say.

Not long after, under cover of day.
Belinda and crew stole away.

On my wall, there is a bare spot.
Belinda The Biker still owes me a clock.

ironhorse

they called him
ironhorse
the child
who became
a renegade

he never stayed
in one place
made friends
wherever he went
and travelled
far beyond
anyone he knew
would dare

he had a look
in his eye
kinda lost
kinda sad

i said
i know you like the taste of drink
are you going to settle down one day?

not to worry
he said
i'm a solitary guy
i know where i'm going
and
i do as i please

mother, he said
she's messin' with my mind

he left for
a long time
called now and then
over the years

one day
he showed up
unexpectedly
he said
home's a good place
to rest

not long after
ironhorse left again
now he travels
among the stars

for Brian

Jane Inyallie

the forgotten son

I

the forgotten son
stands alone
in a crowd of youth

he searches
the faces
of those around him
looking for
something
that lies
beyond
his reach

he fades
into
arcades
pool halls
all night bars
and corner cafes

the street
becomes
the only home
he knows or wants
he fights
anyone
or anything
that stands
in his way

he boozes
drugs

and smokes
until
nothing satisfies
his appetite
not even
the SM girls
who knowingly
travel the night
he roams
the streets
and avenues
snarling
yelling
and screeches
down alleys
into the night

II

the forgotten son
is older now
he's tired
of the highs
and the lows
there's no more
excitement
in the fight

he no longer looks
at the faces
of those around him

he looks
at his reflection
and sees
where

Jane Inyallie

he's been
and
he knows
where he's going

tears run
down his
stubbled cheeks
when he realizes
he
is
his father's
son

Jane Inyallie

the line

most of us
know
when
we've crossed the line
and
we don't
know
what it's like
until
we've crossed it

if
you can see
the line
it's easier
to get back

the further
away
you go
the harder
it is
to get back

when
you can't see
the line
anymore
you start
to forget
it's
there

Terminal Frost 1.

<u>puck on ice</u>

first winter in Ontario
first time playing hockey on ice

bunch of local boys
on a frozen pond

hack the puck around
out of bounds

over the snowbank to get it
foot goes through the ice

all the way up to my knee
water so cold

quickly pulled out my foot
told them about the thin ice

just laughed at me
found it funny

laughed along with them
slapped that puck around on the ice

Terminal Frost 2.

floating in the dead sea

five Native people decide to float in the dead sea
to hang out and sunbathe
an absolutely beautiful day to float
to float

found a good spot to put our blankets
head down to the water's edge
gaze over the water
awe-struck

on the other side of the lake of salt
is the country of Jordan
it felt like we were in heaven
oh in heaven

awesome sight of the landscape
smell of salty air
forever etched into our memories
stepped the rest of the way into the dead sea
amazed at how one floats with such ease
exerting no energy
enjoying the clear blue sky

a mud bath that covers the entire body
dark clay mud baked on the skin by the sun
back to the lake to wash it off
(glorious)
feeling refreshed, revitalized
clean life energy
five native people said good bye to the dead sea

Terminal Frost 3.

young boy swimmer

young boy swimmer
swims at jone's beach
for about a hour

young boy swimmer decides
to swim to a friend's home
just down the
shore line a ways

swims closer to the dock
weeds the thick weeds
twine and wrap themselves
around young boy swimmer

more he struggles
more the weeds tighten
around young limbs
hysteria and panic strike

young boy swimmer
has no breath
at that moment he is
submerged under water

looking up from under the water
fights to free himself
thoughts of dying
terrify young boy swimmer

message to "save yourself"
was enough to save his own life
weeds loosen enough
release young boy swimmer

Terminal Frost 4.

<u>alone with myself</u>

isolated in this one spot out in the deep woods
overcast weather on the day
hadn't started to rain until an hour ago
alone with myself

no place to live
in a mental mess
had my health at least
alone with myself

decided to run from myself
to have my troubles disappear
if only for a little while
alone with myself

thought about what I should do
the song New Machine
plays in my ears
I have always been here
I have always seen through these eyes
alone with myself

rain turned into a steady down fall
stayed right where I was under the tree
didn't want to leave this safe shelter
alone with myself

carved a cross of all things to do
soothed and complimented this sad feeling
alone with myself

Jack D. Forbes

New Age of Circuses

Make us laugh
Make us cry
Make us forget that it's a
World of Entertainment
Sensory addictions
Circuses
Overwhelming even our homes
Television's fungus-like
Growth and we are grasped with
Octopusian tentacles of desire.

A stream of ice cream cones and
Hot dogs and candy bars
Apples it carries
Laced with glass and strychnine,
Mixed with snot and faeces
Blood and guts, the
Poisons of violence, brutality,
Self-centered narcissism,
Love of filthy lucre layering
Sentimentality and just plain
Sex.

Good it all seems,
Tsunami of
Distractions, of education, of
Armchair travel, of exploring
Nature but its sheer volume
Suffocating to the many
Who cannot say no.

Entertainment's world is not
About goodness though, nor

High-minded romance,
Selling instead our
MINDS and our time
Highest bidder gets them.

Because when we
Surrender to being enter-tamed
Addicts, we become slaves,
Pimps to the
Corporations, organizations, and
Politicians who want to
Crap into our
Brain, into our
Emotions, into our reflexes, into our
Deepest private selves

Exposed to every
Imaginable kind of torture,
Murder, rape, watching
Depraved behaviour even by our
Heroes, the cops, the private
Detectives who brutalize people
And make us cheer and
Feel it's normal with the
Selling of sweatshop-made shoes by
Millionaire hoopsters.

Human beings being reduced to the
Ugly banality of the consumer,
Passively fighting
Obesity, their loss of
Authenticity in the couch-potato world
Life's bystander or as a paying
Customer in a work-out room
Desperate to have a
Physical existence.

Immersed in a new
Kind of corporate-fascism
Without armies of black or
Brown-shirted goons since
Television and circus
Pull us into an apolitical
Maze where participation
Means being bamboozled by
Money's lies.

Life for too many of us has become a
Fantasy of pleasure which is
Really pain, a myth of
Being entertained, when we are
Enslaved, really being hypnotized
Until we die of old age,
Lonely in our old people's home, still
Watching TV images flicker before a
Mind already dead!

Un-ending entertainment is a
Social sedative, a
Narcotic worse than cocaine,
Creation of inertial
Indifference to all but the
Shopping mall and the gladiator's
Arena.

Coliseum, mall, boob-tube,
Symbols of a new autocracy,
Demo-Rep one party state
Money is the measure
Of all, and where the celebrated are
Mindless cretins, skinny narcissistic
Models, and actors whose

Being is to imitate,
Not to initiate.

Rome the new has found that
Circuses still work,
Circuses and bread but bread
Means now material
Goods, and for that some will
Steal others
Will give up freedom for the
Chance on the lottery of
Life or the sudden plummeting into
Depths of the under
Class, to be forgotten and
Despised in a world where
Politics is only money
Differently spent.

To be entertained
Great it sounds, doesn't it?
But when they've got you
Hooked by your
Eye-balls, or by your ear-drums,
Or by the boredom of an emptied life
Ask yourself what has been lost.

Could it be you?
The you
That might have been?

Jack D. Forbes

Picasso's Fall

Picasso
        it is told
        did not grow
        older and wiser
        like some Indian Elders
lust
        and delusions of wealth
        travel
        with him
        spiralling downward
        his quest
is not spiritual
        he loses the secret
genius
        he once had obscured
by vanity
        by jet-set
        unrealness

He decays,
        it seems,
        like an old
        rich man

Old men
        especially
        old rich men
        old famous men
        must be
careful
        in chasing
        young women
who is the hunter?
        motives are everything,

and style. . .
The prick
of materialism
erect as it can be
in old age
hardened by self
craving
illusions of being
numero uno
must fail
in the wreckage
of discarded
lovers
beneath the feet
of desire.

Picasso
grateful are we
for the beauty
for the lessons
driven through you
by the World of Spirit
sad
that you did not
at the last
grasp your own
teaching

But then
in the end
we learn
from
both
your genius
and, finally,
your humanity!

Women Made of Earth and Honey

I think a lot about these
                maple-syrup coloured girls
About
                mountain-honey nut-brown ladies
About
                deep, dark molasses women
About
                golden-brown-sugar girls
About
                red-brown earth coloured ladies
About

                rich smelling, soft-hard Mother Earth women
                Her same colours
                all browns and reds
                and blacks.

Giving thanks to Our Creator
                for making
                so many kinds of women-folk
                different shades of brown
                and shapes and sizes
                smelling of sage and pine and wild grasses
Just to satisfy
                my mind.

Brown wood-toned women
                suffering
                strong
                surviving
With little children around them
                bringing forth
                the generations
Our lives passing through
                their
                bodies.

I can't speak of all women
                but these women I know
                Indian
                Black
                Mexican and more

Bending under heavy loads but standing strong
                              these last
                              four hundred years
                              going on still this day
                              lasting and loving
                              nurturing
In calm fierceness
                              making elbow-room
                              for hope
With soft flesh hard as steel.

Native women
                              thousands strong
With beautiful hearts
                              in old cars chugging
                              kids piled high
                              crowded homes and migrant camps
                              no money
Helping kinfolk
                              nursing men and children
                              beaten-down
Warriors and mothers
                              hard and soft
                              strong and gentle
                              singing and laughing
                              with sidelong glances at constant pain.

We shall sing a song
                              for these women
                              the Mockingbird does
                              the Meadowlark
                              and wild canary
                              the wind and I
                              to caress
                              honour
                              and respect
Our hard as iron
                              soft as rabbit's fur
                              women-folk
Caught in a storm
                              they gather the children
                              around them
                              keep us all warm.

Jack D. Forbes

It don't matter where I go

        there's something
        about
        these Earth-Coloured women

Special I mean

        is it the eyes
        the way they look at you?

They like men

        no matter how bad we treat them
        still liking us
        ready to try
        after every disappointment
        to take us in again
        bits of themselves given freely
        If we give something back
            they grow stronger
        And so do we.

Something special

        I tell you
        about these Indian girls
        dancing proud
        singing high nasal style
        holding babies in their arms
        natural noble ladies
        dignified
        shy and bold
        unafraid
        self-confident
        standing tall

Unless we men help to saw them down.

And Red-Black girls

        Mother America
        Mother Africa
        thrust together by slaver's boats
            and raiders' guns
        making powerful trans-oceanic magic
        from Brazil to Massachusetts

And Black girls

        of many tribes and roots
        forged together
        anvil-hardened

like their sisters
earth-coloured
strong
mean and mellow
calling ancient spirits
with hoodoo eyes
un-named candomble.

Even blind

one can see
these our earth-coloured women
desecrated
denigrated
denied
defamed

Taught to boogie away the pain
'sulted and 'slaved to whoring
boozed and abused

Still with style

but all the while
being destroyed
like jewels ground up
making dust storms
coating men's lungs
with asbestos fibres
of finely-shattered
obsidian and jade

Bits of women

that coughing cannot spit out
shame
and
tears.

Natural

unaffected
un-sophistry-cated
girls from down the country roads
old ways in them still

Around us

making wholeness
in us
curing
healing

with magic of honey and herbs
Medicine-women passing on powers
soul to
soul
a hand on your arm
or touching your hair
a song
a smile.

Tough at twelve
women at sixteen
girls still at fifty
Carrying us all on their backs
laughing and easy while
serious and stubborn
Loving love
moving in unison with their bodies
unashamed of female natures
juicy and sweet, not dry and sour
deep feelings nurtured, not crushed
many-dimensioned women,
not cold and calculating minds
Sharing the universal pain
dancing the dance
that leads
to our healing.

Undulating sensuous bodies
restrained two-step forms
Dancing to different music
but dancing still
Dancing right on through
these four hundred years
these twenty generations
of hostile glances
hateful looks
crocodile smiles
rocks and guns

"So sorry, we just hired someone"

"So sorry, we just rented our last apartment—
just forgot about the sign"
of a scowl mouth smiling.

Looking into your own being
                        Your own mirror
                        You see a true reflection—
How beautiful you really are!
                        Oppressor's mirrors
                        like fun-house glass
                        only distorts and warps—
                        do not look there for images!

With the mirror of my gut and being
                        exaltation you will see
Exalting high
                        these brown and black girls
                        putting them elevated on a sacred hill
                        giving them regal titles
                        for all of the contests
                        they've won
                        though no one wanted them
                                to enter
                        but kept out
                                they still win
                        hands-down
                                anyway.

Third World women-folk
                        growing up in the back
                        of a fast-moving
                        pick-up truck
                        out in the rain
                        all wet and cold,
                        hungry
                        still with love to give
                        calm
                        with a song
                        they nurture
                        rebound
                        find joy
                        where others find only
                                misery and
                                self-pity.

Surely you have won
                        every reward
                        a man

can give.

Daughters of *Yemanha*

of Changing Woman
of *Kwan-Yin*
of *Isis*
of *Oxum*
of White Buffalo-Calf Woman

Your browness is a visible sign
of the sweet honey
and enduring earth
from which
You have been formed
and of your nature,
which is Sacred.

Burying My Mother

Death sits on my doorstep
Knows me
Passes a greeting
My heart does not understand.

Death sits on the edge
Of the living,
Peeling off the skin
Of the wind,
Until it sounds hollow,
Emptied of its shells.

Hollow like the swift air
Rushing through
The veins of the Badlands
At night when the ancient voices
Rise against human ears.

It remembers the veins of the day too,
Emptying them
Off their blood—
Silent veins of days
Lying on the earthen floor,
Rattling in the hollow wind, trembling
Before the darkest sunrise.

My Answer to the Professor
Who Said I Should Write More Like a Man to Be Any Good

When I write
I can breathe
out dreams
inside my skin.

They flow out of my lips
like sounds of love on the tongue
disappearing into thin air

appearing again on the paper,
delicately arranged flowers
slowly coming into view
at the first hint of my sunrise.

Touching the new light of day.
Softly moving through
the lines of our doors
we keep so closed.

As if we could stop creation
of all these things in our lives
instead of painting their voices
their words, under our blood,
listening to their smoky whispers
caressing our bones,
dancing with all their powers
in the open sky.

On Trying to Make Chit Chat at Dinner

Tell me, he says
of your heart's desire
I will give it to you.

I want what you
cannot give me
I say.

How do I explain home?

The home I find
in slits, cracks, slivers
of light between
the teeth of the day

where God meets me
walks my inner earth
listens to my stones inside me
touches those small rock creviced places,

turning my heart
into a blazing red sun
burning the sky
burning the world
burning into eternity.

Zuya Wiyan

I grow old in the dark
Ancient, like the spiralling winds
On Hambleceya

I long for the unseen
To go into the Hills of the Forgotten
Watch the prairie flow beneath my eyes.

Only people make me lonely.

I am home here, in the place
Where the spirits bring the new day,
The small circle of blazing fire
Calling

Us to live, to place our lips
On the curved brightness
With all the passion
Of each everlasting breath,
Calling us to touch
The bones of God,
To touch the fingertips
Of Tunkasila.

Nagi Zuya Mani

In the darkness
Of a hollow room
Standing in the sun
Against city traffic
Against people running
The wrong way
Saying the Earth is flat,
I see those haunting eyes
Within me my demon
Does not whisper my name
He roars
Tearing my heart
Into shredded meat
Before dawn.

I am lost, unable to walk
Tired of knowing darkness in the trees
Facing yellow eyes.
This moment I am alone—
It helps to have company
When you sit in black nests.
To see what your own
Demons have to teach you.

The problem is
You must meet them, speak
Their language
Or the language of God;
They know both. But the tongue
You use must be your own.
You must choose
To sit with yellow pain
When no one else notices

Too busy they are
Falling off the edge of the Earth.

I had become arrogant,
Thinking my own demon battles
Were victories, disappearing
Into the summer sun, bent
And faded like a warm sword.

And now, my demon hisses
Asking me about metal,
About sunlight,
if I still see Beauty in all things.
I answer
the darkness does not own me
Although I have come to know
Its language, the names of its birds
Flying in the silent wind
Yet, God is near,
And you are here to remind me
Only That the Earth is round.

Thrown Away

As soon as they had finished loading the trucks, the new staff sergeant yelled: "Flak jackets and helmets. Get 'em on. This is still Indian country." And although the heat was a suffocating presence, a humid oven, they put their five-pound helmets back on and their half-inch thick flak jackets, too. Joseph noted the muck on his boots, dried now and flaking like very old paint. He felt the sweat rolling off him. Earlier, he had smashed his thumb, and it hurt. All Joseph wanted—all any of them wanted—was to get on a truck and to get moving, to catch a little bit of breeze.

The order came to saddle up, and they did, collecting their gear and scrambling onto the waiting deuce and a halfs, not talking much, too hot and too tired even for grab-ass. The more ambitious among them moved a few cases of the C-rations they had loaded and made places to sit; the others just plopped down wherever they could. The short convoy turned east out of the compound, toward the larger road that would carry them north. As it happened, Joseph had jumped into the truck that had taken the lead—if it had been after dark, he would have been ordered into it, anyway, since the staff sergeant believed he could see in the dark.

"I'm mixed-blood, not full-blood," Joseph had protested, not wanting more than his share of guard duty and time out on point.

"Do the math, Private," the staff sergeant had countered. "If you see only half as good as a regular Indian, you can still see twice as good as these other guys." He made a gesture that took in the marines all around them.

Joseph could not believe such stupidity. It was simply too ludicrous. Joseph had thought about putting in for a transfer—he had thought of other things, too—but had concluded that his time was so short that the most direct route was just to get through—the means to which altered then, too:

Joseph had seen very clearly every single man in his squad busily looking away.

For a few minutes they bumped along, sweat drying, thankful for the twenty-mile-per-hour breeze. Then, just before they turned onto the north-south road, the truck slowed to a crawl. One by one they stood up to see what was the matter. Most every one of them made a comment; every comment made was foul-mouthed.

The ragged column of refugees stretched out of sight. The driver didn't bother to honk—there were just too many to move with a horn. They took up the whole road and then some. The lucky ones were packed into carts that ranged from primitive to prehistoric. An old woman rode in a makeshift farm wagon, an injured child on a crude sled. Most simply walked, their eyes dull and fixed straight ahead. Away to the north was the sound of an ongoing aerial bombardment.

"Well," DJ said, taking out his well-honed Ka-Bar and slashing open a carton of C-rats, "we might as well make the best of it." He dug around until he found a can of cake and another of peaches; but no sooner had he put the cans on the roof of the cab and started to open them than kids began to appear.

"Hey! Hey, GI Joe!" an older boy yelled, and banged against the side of the truck. "Hey!"

"Hey what, you little fuck?" the squad leader snapped in reply. He was tall and lean with long, ropey muscles and a country boy's hands with big knuckles. If the boy saw the squad leader's M-16 swing in an arc that included him, he wasn't put off by it.

DJ took out a pilfered mess-hall spoon and began to eat his cake and peaches, smacking his lips with obvious enjoyment.

The squad leader slung his rifle across his back and tore at the case of C-rations DJ had cut open. He stood up with four olive-green cans, three in one hand and one in the other. He flipped the single can in the air, up and down, hefting it between the short tosses, weighing it. By now more kids had come; they walked beside the slow-moving truck, waving, shouting, holding their hands out for food. The truck stopped for a moment, the driver irritably sounded the horn, the kids pushed into a bunch, and the squad leader wound up and threw.

The heavy can caught the boy over the eye, and he crumpled right where he stood, collapsing as if his strings had been cut all at once.

The younger kids laughed and scrambled after the can as it ricocheted. Two smaller boys pushed a taller one forward as a shield. Others got so excited they tried to climb over each other's backs. The squad leader stretched his lips into a thin, hard expression, looked around at the men, then threw again.

For a moment, no one in the truck moved. DJ even stopped eating. Joseph watched warily. Then, as if on signal, blades flashed, and very nearly every one of them tore into the cases of C-rations and the smaller boxes inside. They ripped out the cans and started throwing them, fruit cocktail, peaches, lima beans, meats of all sorts.

The cans flew flat and hard.

The kids who were hit solidly dropped like the first one, but the others kept coming even after their giggling and laughing stopped. Some limped from a hit in the leg; others cradled an arm or a hand. A young girl stood feeling her teeth—a second can missed her by inches.

What impressed Joseph most was the calm and quiet, the orderliness of it. There were grunts of exertion as the men in the truck loosened up and threw harder. There were thuds and thumps and ugly, wet, soft-tissue sounds as the cans struck, but the children seemed afraid to make any sound and any sound they did make they muffled. Joseph didn't care to join in, but he didn't object to it, either—it just wasn't what he would call fun. Idly, he reached into an open case and pulled out a can, but, because he just sat there with it, it was grabbed from his hand. So he watched, and as he did so he wondered when his feelings about refugees had evolved to such passive indifference. It still irritated him that they so often got in the way. He still found them pathetic and resented the many problems they created. That they were outsiders in their own country should, it seemed to him, create some sympathy, but it didn't—not even when he recalled those hand-lettered signs in Oklahoma that read, "No Injuns"; not even when he replayed the conversation with the staff sergeant and caught the wink that had passed between him and his favourite corporal. The refugees had become all but invisible—his feelings for them as insubstantial as ghosts.

Suddenly, a single shot cracked, and the men throwing froze; the kids still clamoured after the cans.

Likely, it was all the time he had spent on point and on the perimeter at night, but Joseph had his rifle shouldered and sighted at the sound even before the whole sound had passed. There was a slight *snick* as he pushed off the safety.

"Cut that silly shit out," the staff sergeant yelled angrily from the truck right behind them. Then he locked eyes with Joseph who was looking calmly at him down the barrel of his M-16 stubby. The staff sergeant's voice cracked just a little when he added, "We need those supplies for ourselves."

The men in the truck sat down again, two or three looking a little sheepish. Joseph leaned back on a single, low C-ration case, knees higher than butt, arms over knees, rifle cradled snugly between hands and feet. He examined his thumb, which felt worse than it looked. His arms, he saw, were tanned. They had the same bronzed, coppery-red colour he had always admired on his grandfather, a colour on the old man unaffected by exposure to the sun. His grandfather was dead now, but, as always, it was that unique colour that Joseph thought of when he defined for himself the primary difference between the pure and the mixedblood, the colour and whether or not it had to be renewed by the sun, the colour and who walked and who rode the trails marked by tears, the colour that let him step across borders as if he could see in the dark.

Magic Carpets

Three in one
Three in one
Three in one

She worked
The rags
Into braids
That laid
As carpet
Beneath our feet

One by one
One by one

She ripped
by hand
Colourful bands
Sewn into one
Her gifts
Of love

Bigger
Bigger still
A ball
Of braid
Would appear
Like magic
Attaching
To canvas

Thread knotted
Fingers twisted
Whistling while
She worked
Songs of
The old country

Covering, covering
Cold floors
Spreading, spreading
She made more
Multi-coloured
Surfaces of braids
Easing steps
Her time
She paid

Braided flooring
Telling stories
Of a
Worker
A woman
A queen

Her legacies
Still cushion
Our steps
Though thin
And old
We have kept
Her braids
Another day

She is done. . .
Three into one
Three into one
Three into one

No Reservation

I am an Indian, without reservation
Without memory of a land
Where my ancestors lie sleeping
My blood does not show traces
Of the crops raised there
And my accent does not say
I am part of that tribe.

No, I was born and raised
Away from them, away from there.
Our sufferings, the same
Our lessons, equal
I look to them, who have remained
Part of that territory
And see a mirror image looking back

I learn from them, and they from me
I need their past to know me more
A fresh breath is breathed into the language, the culture
As I ask and inquire
Of a way of life, in jeopardy of death

No, my upbringing does not recall
Kidnapping to institutions
Of sadness of a language lost, I never had.
And I share all the same
The skin I walk in, and brown black eyes
That house ancient secrets unrevealed even to me.

An Indian is an Indian, is an Indian
We are the true travellers of more than one world
Your journey is my journey, and mine is yours
This we share, in this granule of time

I know my brothers and sisters by the way we feel.
The enemy can look similar, so trust your ancient instincts

There is an indescribable joy
In returning to a land, meant for you by blood
I embrace all that it is
For this . . . I have no reservation

Kim Shuck

Because the Feet of Four Indian Women Might Change the Weather on the East Coast

*For any of the Indian
kids I know who went
off to Harvard and found it a cold
place.*

Dancing on this slightly uneven ground,
We circle with the fire always on our right.
Our feet are the accurate feet
Of southern style traditional dancers.
We place them very carefully
Each time we take
Small steps
To the music.

We are pink and blue and green and dark brown.
Our hair is braided
And decorated
According to individual equations.
Nothing is left to chance.

We are connected by the
Drum.
The fringes on our shawls shift
In exact patterns
They describe the movement
Of turbulent water or
The stars.

Our feet hold a message too.
They say:
We are proud
Proud
Proud
Proud of you.

Some Things I Know About Love that Might be of Some Use

1.

I cannot take a handful of dirt from my backyard without seeing a woman.
She has a crooked left eyetooth, solid hips and thighs
And hair that reaches to her knees.
When she tips her head back she can feel her hair
Caressing her calves, the small of her back.
I can see her gathering cress here
Some four hundred years ago.

I have to wonder with each handful of dirt
What part of this dirt contains her hair?

As I plant my squash
I am grateful
That she cares for me in this way.

2.

I have heard the old women say
That the children look like the parent
Who had the most fun making them.

I wonder at the curl in my hair
And my grandmother's story of the escaped slave
Taken in
And loved so intensely
By her great-grandmother
That the erotic aftershock
Curls the hair of one member of the family
Per generation
Ever since.

3.

Sometimes I see a flash of gold brown light
In someone's eye.
And I smell the flooded pecan grove
Near grandma's house.
I wonder if this is what it is for salmon
Swimming upstream.
Some small taste of the familiar
That sets their sense of direction.

And I think about my father
With a shiver for the bravery
Of trusting someone else's sense of direction.

4.

Some things are more important than the time they take.

5.

This scrubby grey mint
Was snatched from death
On a hot day near Petaluma.
It rode in a wet tissue
All the way to San Francisco.
And despite only having had
Half an inch of root
It flourishes.

Home Songs

1.

Always consider the possibility that you take yourself too seriously.

2.

That dry cleaner is built
On the most sacred spot
In four counties.

It was not intended as an act of irreverence.
They didn't ask and we
Were too embarrassed for them
To say.

Yeah, sometimes I get angry.
Most often when
I can't find any dirty laundry
So I can go pray.

3.

Just 'cause you don't know the stories,
Doesn't mean there aren't any.

4.

It's been ten years since I was home, but
Jake doesn't even look up from the paper
As I enter his store.
"Your Gram is out of flour.
You want tea you have to buy it.
Milk's probably soured."

I love you too old man.

5.

Humour and food are the trickiest
Of cultural artifacts,
But overlaps do occur.

My Polish and Tsalagi relatives
Sat down one evening and enjoyed
Potato pancakes together.

And then there was the afternoon
Of near delirium:
28 Elderly Indians
Listening to Seuss in translation.

Larry Nicholson

Residing Poem

I

808 SPILLER ROAD S. E. (1997)

up early
cold cereal with Canada AM
or cartoons
the screen door slams,
as the schoolyard awaits

grey skies
over stockyards down the street
carry the stench
of fermenting malt and slaughter

two blocks away
a train blares its approach
but nobody wakes
or hears anything out of the ordinary

at the bus stop
Jimmy the Lush lies fetal
and waits for his ride to the tank,
or heaven,
whichever comes first
and not that he'd know the difference

I am the only Indian boy I know
and invisible
to old men with bulbous noses
who hold up crumpled newspapers
to hide the evidence
of another failure,
ragged and dishevelled men

trying to forget
a lifetime on the sly

the winds of change don't blow here,
they just laugh and spread the smell

II

RESERVATION #341 (1990)

imperceptibly,
night descends over twilight
as the rise and slope
of this country
meet somewhere beyond
the dark blue and black
calm, humid air hints of promise
my senses are piqued
by warm tea
and the life teeming
in the meadow behind this,
my uncle's house,
a breath of wind
delivers the scent of horses
and sweet blades bending there

like the people who live here,
fireflies hover and dart without pattern
their bodies brilliant
points of illumination

in other field,
a young girl holding a jar snares one
and watches as the fly struggles to breathe
she walks away bored
as light from the body fades
then disappears

promised land

my name is nothing
my age means less

i come from all countries
where there are no boundaries
no judgements
only clarity and stillness
broken by a squeal of delight
as she learns how to squeeze my hand

from us come her first words
old words with ancient meanings
we search for those meanings
unconcerned with success or failure

we accept our station
without question or destination
all places are young
and the wind never blows cold

in her mother's arms
at times
is all the beauty i can take

sleeping well in the knowledge
that we are safe
i am home

Larry Nicholson

Steal My Thunder

I listened
as right before she hung up,
she said "I love you,
and don't ever come back."

Damn!

That was my last quarter, too.

coyote dreamz & rocks

met her over there,
eye suppoze?

cha.

whut happind?

said he dream'd
abowt coyote
and rocks

what kind of rocks?

oh, the blue ones and red ones
and maybee one night yell-oh
he thinkx

so now where is
our neffew?

bye the river
ficksing a fire—
you know
he ses she's sen-say-shun-al*!*
and she frah-lix
like nobuddy's bizness,

izzat right?

and he alreddy lit the rocks
the blue and red ones,
prob'ly even the yellow

Larry Nicholson

betch it's got
sumthing to doo with colours—
always duzz with hym,
even seez colours in the dark, him

c'mon, better get,
help'em ficks that swet

still,
it's sumthing
to wonder abowt
you know what they say,
after coyote dreamz
nuthings ever the same

cha

cha

Identity Crisis

Part I

from your grandparents
You are an Indian

from an Indian
You are not Indian

from a Métis
Métis are Indian

from a Halfbreed
Métis are not Indians

from an Aboriginal
You are White

from a Caucasian
You are not White

from a Non-Status Indian
You are of Aboriginal Status

from a Status Indian
You are not Status

from a North American
You are Canadian

from an Elder
You are not Canadian

from a Nish cousin
You are Native

from a White cousin
You are not Native

from yourself
You are?
You are not?
. . . ?

I Know Who I Am

Part II

from my grandmother
who spoke of the Seven Fires
spoke her own language
of coming together as a nation
to feast to talk to pray
from my grandmother who told me
I am an Indian

from an Indian Warrior Woman
who I made arrangements to interview
over the phone seemed welcome
to meet a Cree/Anishinaabe/Métis
but at the meeting her smile dropped
and breath stilled
at the shake of my hand
seemingly unnerved by my fair skin
or perhaps my blue/grey eyes
she recoiled in avoidance
not sharing her warrior stories for my interview
in her own way she told me
you are not an Indian

from a Métis dancer dressed with sash and beads
beaming joy at the indoor pow-wow
who danced his grandfather's heritage
danced his mother's pride
from the Métis dancer defending his beliefs
who laughed at me and claimed
you are an Indian you are Métis

from the white racist
sitting in the greasy spoon
itching for a bone to pick

descends upon me and my Uncle
"listen up you lazy lot
the past is over so quit your complaining
you otta' pay taxes like the rest of us"
from this misanthropic man
"You're not White, You're a no good Indian"

snow white in winter, I could easily mix, mingle and meld my
way into the mainstream, walk in the White world and I would
never have to debate or ponder it again. except that I tried, I
tried to assimilate my ass right into their houses and
relationships and offices but I just couldn't breathe the stale air
or laugh at the foreign jokes or settle into the form and
thinking that creates people like that, people that I never fit in
with no matter how good my acting or how much I bit my
tongue and nodded my head and smiled and pretended to agree
or understand, I just did not belong

back where it's brown and I understand the thinking because
that's where I come from, back with the skins of my same skin,
of my roots, where it smells like home and I can breath the
thick delicious air, I get accused of not being Enough, not the
same and any faults I may have are always reflected back to
my being too White.

where am I supposed to go?

what if I die and go to White heaven
will I have to eternally sit on the sidelines alone
where will all my ancestors be?

what if I die and my spirit turns
into a wolf and I finally fit into a place of unity
will I still get to say goodbye to my mom?

I am tired of comparing knowledge
I am tired of dissecting the family tree

baking bannock does not make you an Indian
diluted blood does not make you White
from my grandmother
who told me
you are Indian
from my grandmother
who told me
in her own language
of seven fires
who told me
of a revolution
who told me
things are going to get worse before they get better
lest we come together as a nation
to feast and talk and pray
from my grandmother in her wisdom
I know who I am

William George

Mountain Bedded Rock

Along the Stanley Park seawall, I stroll this spring morning,
From across the Burrard Inlet, I etch myself out of the
mountainside.
My image is captured there once,
Every line through the contours of the Grouse Mountain.

I can argue that we are rock.
We always have been.
Composed of earth and minerals,
The Creator made us out of stone and dirt.

I forget that I am rock.
And when the mountain slides to the ocean,
That is not my concern.

I pull myself away from my place here,
Even denying that the world shaking
And falling apart has anything to do with me.

In the blue green of this world,
Sing and pray with me
As we re-create ourselves in the mountain.

I stand here on the seawall,
With the wind blowing in from the ocean,
I know that the foundation of who we are
and why we are here is that you and I,
We are mountain bedded rock.

My Pledge

I pledge allegiance to this here collective,
We who live and breathe Indigenous rhythm.
And the dream voices echo our prayer hymn,
To harmonize with life forces is not selective.
For we are responsible to be protective,
Ever strive to nurture others, her and him.
For us to breathe life into words is no whim.
We walk-speak a language demonstrative.

For witnesses, my honour and respect do I pledge.
I am a writer standing here sharing with the universe.
I speak the words that move powerful through me,
With my pen to the page, my words cut the edge.
I challenge the form prose, script, poetry, even verse.
The words' rhythm is my expression that I set free.

William George

Sockeye Salmon Dream

sockeye salmon dream
seeps into my bones flesh
the west coast rain sings

Life Line

I hold Mother gently as she draws in her last breaths. They are slow and quiet, faint against the soft rippling waves of the stream that runs beside us. We have lived here for many years and now I feel her life slipping away as I watch her dry lips tremble with every thought that goes through her mind. Her head, nestled on my lap, dangles silken grey and white strands of hair onto cool green grass leading down to the stream. Her quiet words ripple:

"Take me to water
running over land.
Take and put me so my feet feel
gentle tickling rushes of wetness.

Hold my hand and place it
just under the folding surface
to feel the rocks that mold
the beauty of the stream.

I want to feel the tumble
of thirst quenching sweetness
flowing over land alongside
evergreens and red willows.

Take my body and place it
gently into the water
so that I may course
along the same path.

I want the streams to carry me
to big river currents
that plunge mightily
into James Bay."

If I could, I would turn myself into a stream and safely carry Mother's silent body to the quiet bed of salt water. But I can only follow alongside the gentle rush of the stream while songs of tree sparrows sing gracefully in rhythm to her journey. Bull rushes give way to boulders as the stream becomes a river. Mighty flooding folds of water cascade over land. Rapids drown the songs of trees sparrows. Only at pools and broad river beds do I hear their sweet songs as the river volume rises and falls. The white brown blue green torrents of water rush out of the river's mouth. The pace lessens. The roar diminishes. Song sparrows' words fade into seagulls' cries. The stream has come to rest in James Bay's lulling cradle of salt water. White grey seagulls swoop down to catch a glimpse of themselves, occasionally penetrating the mirror of wet glass, buoyed by the silent body of water. The glass cracks momentarily as seagulls' eyes guide their beaks to their prey. Minnows are scooped up by sharp beaks, swallowed whole and slide down slippery throats to energize sinewy muscles. Sinewy muscles made strong by traveling morning skies, which after a storm is wrapped in a sky blanket of brilliant light yellow with a hint of pink. It is here where mother comes to rest.

In a casket of water
she silently floats with
pale yellow flowers
cradled in her hands.

Blankets of waves splash
gently against her frail body
as slow currents swirl
her grey white hair
in gentle strands
about her head.

Breasts once full
of life-giving milk
now fold in wrinkles
from her chest.

Lips that once
kissed pain better
no longer breathe
the fresh scent of
pink Twin Flowers growing
under giant spruce trees
that dance along
the shores of James Bay.

Margaret Orr

Green Light, Red Light

wide and fast
around the corner of a building
to fall at the feet of a suit
that happens to be going in the same direction
you are but in a different way
you scramble to the hot dog stand
by the bus stop a woman stands
with her head stooped over her purse
she reaches in and change falls silently
on the grass by the garbage
where you always reach down
hard and fast over to food
before he changes his mind not to accept
the little change that shows what you have
been through ever since
you came to the city
from your reservation home
to watch street lights change colour
while neon lights flicker
and reflect the same stars
somewhere in the recesses
of your memory

Trophy Room

Look at me

don't just pick me up blindly 'cause
my face has been burnt by the sun

real close.

Hold me and

though my breasts sag from
milk gone dry

turn me around for a long time.

Run your hands down

and my legs show veins that have
popped out from the weight of my children

my spine and my thighs.

Stroke my wrists and

my feet are too big like the
base of a trophy with

skinny ankles.

Margaret Orr

Turn me over and

scars of survival mark
my hands and my back

read what I am made of.

Keep me off the shelf

ignore all the wear and tear that hides
the tenderness that created me

to wrap in warm reds and yellow.

Geronimo's Grave

On that dreadful labour day weekend, just a few weeks ago, I got out of the cool air-conditioned car into the hot dry air of Fort Sill, Oklahoma.

As I walked down the path of the Indian Cemetery—prisoners of war of a hundred years before—I thought about the story my little butterfly told me, about the time they visited Geronimo's grave, about the incident where her step-dad had to kill a poisonous snake with a cross because it was after the children.

The grave with two huge juniper trees stood like sentinels—a door to the spirit world. I saw bandanas tied to the boughs of the great ones. There were also offerings in memory of deceased relations. A baby's soother hung still in the desert-like heat.

I pulled from my pocket the purple, blue and pink silk scarf that was once a gift from me to the mother of my daughter. It was my daughter's most cherished possession after her mother had given it to her.

I tied that beautiful scarf to the tree and tears rolled down my cheeks as I prayed. Then I walked away from Geronimo's grave and let go of her spirit.

In her loving and prayerful way, she was a great warrior.
She is now our eldest sister.

White Picket Fences

In town the houses boxed in
with their tiny little boards
neatly nailed together.
Rows upon rows of streets, and homes.
Green grassy lawns, paved driveways and two-car garages.

Out on the Indian Reservation,
A dilapidated residential school,
cemetery and old church,
The dry cracked paint, so brittle it falls.
Only the dust blows freely in the wind.

A space, a plot, a garden, a yard,
All closed in, suffocating,
Eroding the freedom.
The white picket fence stands tall.

Abused Mothers Wounded Fathers

I kept my mother and father
longer than most Indians my age.
I was 41 when she died
and 42 when he drifted away.

Yet sometimes
I despair
how I'd wasted all that time
I never got to know them
until long after they'd gone.

Even from a distance
I think I always knew my mother loved me,
but I used to wonder about my dad,
being as close to him as I was
it was hard to tell.

It must have been hard on them,
how I stay away,
kept all shut up inside,
never married
never gave them grandbabies
to redeem themselves on.
I heard dad tell it once
that he figured it was his fault
how I grew to mistrust the world.

It makes me ache inside
to think about it.
Sometimes I wake
in the middle of the night
and I tell them
things I never told them in life.

Vera Manuel

It's easier for me to talk to them
when they can't answer back.

Mom and dad grew up in residential school.
There wasn't much love in those places.

When I lie very still,
close my eyes
I picture them
as children,
five and six years old.
I take them up into my arms,
hold them tightly,
rock them gently,
kiss them
all over their faces,
the way babies ought to be kissed,
because I know there was no one
to do that for them
back then.
It's somehow soothing to me.

Anishinaabikwe-**Everywoman**

While he *Inini*
>Indian man who seeks the Great Spirit
>looks longingly out the window
>past the birds and trees
>into his own mind
>long hair hiding his back

I *Ikwe*
>Indian woman so close to Mother Earth
>protect him from this cruel and mundane life
>with hard work
>>courage
>>>and love
>my strengths
>while my feet never leave the ground.

My quest never began,
and his will never end.

Linda LeGarde Grover

Chi-Ko-ko-koho and the Boarding School Prefect, 1934

From my owl's nest home, unsteady greasy oak
covered by cowhide long oblivious
to claws tough and curving as old tree roots
I breathe the night breeze, starry broken glass.

I am *Chi-Ko-ko-koho*. My black-centered
unblinking owl eyes see past the dark
growl of this old bear den of a bar,
through stinging fog of unintended
blasphemy, tobacco's tarry prayers
stuck and dusty on a hammered tin ceiling,
to grieving spirits mirrored by my own.
I am *Chi-Ko-ko-koho*, young among owls
as young among lush crimson blooms of death
is the embryonic seedling in my chest,
the rooting zygote corkscrew in my chest,
these days all but unseen, a pink sea spray
sunset on a thick white coffee cup.
My grieving spirit hardly notices
though, in this old bear den of a bar.

My owl head turns clear round when I see him.
I am *Chi-Ko-ko-koho*, I blink away
smoke and fog, my head swivels back
and he's still there, the prefect. He's still there.
He's real, not some ghost back to grab my throat
again with those heavy old no-hands of his
or crack my brother's homesick skinny bones
on cold concrete tattooed by miseries
of other Indian boys who crossed his path.

To the darkness of this bear den of a bar
he's brought his own sad spirit for a drink.

I am *Chi-Ko-ko-koho*, but who he sees
is *Kwiiwizens*, a boy bent and kneeling
beneath the prefect's doubled leather strap,
and *Kwiiwizens* I am. My belly feels
a tiny worm the colour of the moon
writhe in laughter at my cowardice
as that reeking, ruined wreck, the old prefect
step-drags, step-drags his dampened moccasins
to my end of the bar. The flowers weep
above his toes in mourning for us all.

He asks me for a nickel for a beer.
With closed eyes *Kwiiwizens* waits for the strap.

Chi-Ko-ko-koho dives from his grimy perch
to yank the apparition by the hair,
then flies him past the blind face of the moon
to drop him in the alley back behind
the dark growl of this old bear den of a bar.

Indizhinikaaz Kwiiwizens,
gaye indizhinikaaz Chi-Ko-ko-koho.
Ni maajaa. Mi-iw. I leave him there.

I am *Chi-Ko-ko-koho*. I leave him there
under stars of broken glass. I leave him there.

Linda LeGarde Grover

Grandmother at Mission School

Left on smooth wooden steps to think
about disobedience, and forgetfulness
she feels warm sun on the back of her neck
as she kneels on the pale spot worn
by other little girls' tender sore knees,
a hundred black wool stockings
grinding skin and stairs,
beneath one knee a hard white navy bean.

Small distant lightening flickers
pale flashes down her shins, felt by other
uniformed girls marching to sewing class
waiting for their own inevitable return
to the stair, to think and remember what happens
to girls who speak a pagan tongue.

Try to forget this pagan tongue.

Disobedient and forgetful she almost hears
beyond the schoolyard
beyond the train ride
beyond little girls crying in their small white beds

her mama far away
singing to herself as she cooks
and speaking quietly to Grandma as they sew
the quilt for Mama's new baby
and laughing with her sisters
as they wash clothes

the little bean
did it hurt?

"*Bizaan, gego mawi ken*, don't cry"
She moves her knee so the little bean
would feel just the soft part, and not the bone
how long can I stay here?
and when Sister returns to ask if she's thought
she says yes,
I won't talk like a pagan again
and she stands and picks up the little bean
and carries it in her lonesome lying hand
until it's lights out
when the baby bean
sleeps under her pillow.

Linda LeGarde Grover

To the Woman Who Just Bought
That Set of Native American Spirituality
Dream Interpretation Cards

Sister, listen carefully to this.

You'll probably go right past me
when you're looking
for a real gen-yew-whine
Indian princess
to flagellate you a little
and feed your self-indulgent
un-guilt
about what other people
not as fine-tuned and sensitive as you
did to women
by the way, women like me
who you probably go right past
when you're looking.

I know what you're looking for
and I know I'm not it.
You're looking for that other
Indian woman, you want
for a real gen-yew-whine
oshki-traditional princess
and you'll know her when you see her
glibly glinting silver and turquoise
carrying around her own little
magic shop of real gen-yew-whine
rattling beads and jangling charms
beaming about her moon
as she sells you a ticket to her sweat lodge.
She's a spiritual concession stand
and it's your own business, go ahead and buy

or rent it if you want, go ahead
what do I care
acquire what you will,
you've done it before.

I know what you're looking for
and I know I'm not it. Hell, no
I won't be dressing up or dancing for you
or selling you a ceremony
that women around these parts never heard of.
I won't tell your fortune
or interpret your dreams
so put away your money. Hell,
what you really want to buy
you'll never see, and anyway
it's not for sale.

Sister, you weren't listening to this
I know, and I know too that
that authentic, guaranteed
satisfaction or your money back
gen-yew-whine for real
oshki-traditional Indian princess
is easy to find. Bring your cheque book.
Or a major credit card.
I'll be watching you both.

Winona Conceives the Trickster

As a young girl, Nokomis was envied by the stars, who tricked her into falling to earth from her home and mother, the moon. She gave birth to a daughter, Winona, who she loved deeply and sheltered carefully. Winona strayed from her mother while they were out picking potatoes. She was captured in a whirlwind by the North Wind, and became pregnant. Nokomis grieved terribly when the innocent girl died giving birth to Nanaboozhoo.

Trees whistle a warning and look to the sky
as shivering stones dance in liquid blue field,
and listening moccasins warily step
soft up, soft up and a turn, then freeze
as the North Wind seizes the night.
The ice snake winds past Old Woman Moon,
his cloudless stealth feinting gusts of breath,
and shocked stars rue their jealous past
watching First Daughter spin on the edge of the world
as the North Wind takes the night.

Dispelling the Myth of STONEFACE

He was an old man, older than anyone on earth could imagine. He had seen the Indian wars. He saw the women and children turned into slaves. He had watched and waited for the white man to come. He didn't choose to be born an Indian, not in his case. He was the mentor of all time. He had seen other worlds besides earth. He wasn't annihilated, nor was he born into an extinct culture. He was eternal.

As a young boy, he was different than his brothers. He was not permitted to play war games. He was not permitted to speak. No person forbade him, the words would not surface. He was not imprisoned inside himself. He had a connecting spirit, not a grasping spirit but a flowing spirit on a chosen path of determination. The only one that had knowledge of his quest would be the Creator himself.

One morning as he was preparing for the day, he picked up his headband, only today it was for a different reason. He saw the day in front of him and his eyes filled with tears. Blood rushed through his heart with a flush of heat, warming his entire body. He became greatly excited anticipating the day and final sunrise.

The spirit voices became very loud, talking and scurrying to and fro. He knew these people. They were familiar to him. He was remembering he had never spoken a word before now... It had become customary not to speak to anyone without purpose and not to speak to someone without permission.

If people were hungry and the wind was blowing, you could catch the scent of wild game. It was hardly necessary to speak. The warrior hunters would get up at once, jump on their horses to return late afternoon with plenty of sustenance.

The day has passed and it becomes impossible to conceive a circumstance which cannot be realized. This was a strange new world thought the boy. He had captured the dream. He used faith to get him through the day. The only evidence of reality was a sweetly tired body which was his.

"I know you care for me," the young man no longer a boy said to his grandfather with his mind. "Yet I am lonely, who will speak for me? Who will mark my path?" He picked up his moccasins unaware of the time of day, threw his shirt over his shoulder and walked.

The footsteps were new, the grass was soft. He lay down and flew over hard hills, down to lakes. In the wind he heard a song. It was sung by a woman. She is singing to her spirit love. I can't pass this by thought the young man.

Grandfather, I am not like other people but I know I am no different. I don't know why or when I knew or when the realization came. I can talk now, I can sing. I have children but first I teach them with my mind. I teach them the spirit is not fantasy, that life is important without question, that silence is a gift long ago forgotten.

I think the mountains are the real stonefaces, the ones who lie on their ceremonial beds of rock, turned to stone through time, witnessing a forever and eternal adventure of life. I am like those mountains. I want to hear the smallest sparrow rustling in his nest, waiting too for that nourishment, that down to earth daily type of existence.

The man, older now didn't feel so ancient by comparison, and was fortunate never having been compelled to speak, never feeling obligated to explain to another being, something that was beyond him. For words quickly change the meaning in the everlasting traditions of life.

Daughter of the Sun

I entered the din of her silence—she motioned me to sit. Never
taking her eyes from her weaving, the Beloved Woman began
a story.

The sun did not like the people because
such ugly faces were made when they looked at her.
But the moon loved the people
so the jealous sun planned to kill them
and sent scorching rays.
The Little Men turned one of the people
into a rattlesnake to bite and kill the old sun
but the rattlesnake bit the sun's daughter instead.

"I have always wanted to have skin as red as yours," I said to
her, unashamedly.
She continued her work and story.

And when the sun found her daughter dead, she went into hiding
and grieving and all the land was darkened.
The Little Men instructed the people to go to *Tsvsginâ'i*
where they found the daughter of the sun
dancing with the other ghosts.
The people struck her head seven times with a stick
and put her into a box and began to carry her
the long way back to their homes in the East.

I watched as her long hair fell around her shoulders, blending
in with the midnight, moving to Indian time.
On the long journey the daughter of the sun began to plead
with the people to please let her out but they refused.
The Little Men had told them not to open
the box under any circumstances.
But she begged them and begged them,
saying she was really dying,
so they opened the lid of the box
and out flew a red bird to settle in nearby bushes.

"I have waited a long time," I told her. There is but one true path
and I want to know the way.

When the people returned to their homes
and opened the box it was empty.
The sun cried and cried for her daughter
until the people danced and sang
causing the sun to smile and shine through her grief.
Because the people let the daughter of the sun
fly out of the box we cannot bring back the ghosts
of our people from *Tsvsginâ'i*.

Laying down her work, she motioned for me to follow. She
showed me how to touch the future with fingers of intuition
and glimpse the past with guided dreaming. But I could not
capture the total essence of what the Beloved Woman had said
until I began to walk under the waterfalls inside my own
being. Then I began to weave.

NOTES

A Beloved Woman is one who is extremely influential in tribal affairs—a woman who speaks in council meetings and communicates with Beloved Women of other nations. In years past, a Beloved Woman was sometimes known as War Woman because she had the power of life and death over captives of war. She also had a voice in deciding whether or not the Cherokee Nation would go to war.

Little Men—*Anisga'ya Tsunsdi'ga*. The two sons of *Kanati*, the Great Thunder Spirit, who live in the sky vault. Also called the Thunder Boys.

Tsvsginâ'i—The land of the Spirits in the West.

The sun is female to the Cherokee and her brother is the moon.

Rasunah Marsden

The Cunning of Men

everyone I read
writes fancy things
many more intelligent than I
I don't know this
I feel this
the way they understand
so many more things
sooner than I
always intrigues me.

this begins a collection
of stories made from observations
I have made,
some memories are faulty
but as has been pointed out
recently to me,
"things which are important
will come back to you."

when I speak it is easier
but when critical ears are listening
the details of my stories change
though the kernel of the story
may not

but I am here today
to speak a little of these things
& that is all.

an old man of hard experience,
I spent a recent afternoon
appraising a young woman
of the cunning of men.

one day in my teens, I told her,
my mother & I were drunk
& she took me into her bed.
coming to my senses the next day
I beat her severely with a stick.

if something was going well,
I would try to destroy it.
For instance I knew a woman
whose husband was away at war.
I was aware
she had slept with a few men
& eventually it came to be my turn.

news came that her husband was soon
to return but nevertheless I found
her knocking at my door one night.
sending her away, immediately
I phoned her husband & told him
all I knew about his wife's behavior,
which ruined the marriage.

another time I arranged a meeting
in some small town with another woman
I was having an affair with,
proceeded to get drunk & when I came to,
realized the woman was gone.
tho she'd paid my expenses,
& had taken a taxi elsewhere.

I telephoned her to meet me again
& when she arrived she was wearing
sunglasses. when I asked her to take them off,
she showed two black eyes & on her neck
also bruises. "Whoever Beatrice was,
she must have hurt you very badly,"

the woman explained.
I never revealed
my mother's name to her.

years later I confronted my mother
& asked why she had done that
with me & why also she had slept
with other male relatives
I had known. she cried
at what I revealed,
but I forgave her.

stories like these are hard
& sometimes frightening
to digest. But that night
the young woman dreamt
(she told me) that she was talking
to one of the most beautiful
eighteen year olds
she had ever met.

I can only say
there's no explanation
for the hell that people
will go through or be put through,
there's no explanation
why such horrible stories
should be told by a beautiful soul,

but there may often be
a very great distance
between the words you hear
& the inside of the teller.

by contrast, the prettiest words
belie interior selves which are far

from well-intentioned, & far from
something refreshing & healing.

in some mysterious way
it is impossible, I told her,
to find, if you are looking for it,
anything more
than a mixture of evil & purity,
anything more
than fallen ash on snow

Rasunah Marsden

Yellow Leaves

yellow leaves announced premature change
earwigs crowded window sills or fell off countertops
fat flies & then the mosquitoes thinned out drastically
hornets buzzing around the sap of the tree
finally burrowed holes underground as the level of the lake
sank & with it I began yet another year's hibernation

that week my niece called to announce
she'd survived the birth
if not so lustily as her newborn son
& my children's calls quieted one by one
eventually all the curtains were drawn & with them
dreams of the real you still waiting for me
were dreamt in better worlds
in better worlds where the trees were filled
to bursting with yellow leaves that never fell

The Night Charles Bukowski Died

Why did I play the water loud as Herman cried in the shower well two nights ago we took Herman to the field and showed him how to punch kick defend himself and I think of the time we went for lunch at the caf and I said Ho Herman yer sitting the wrong way you can't see the babes if you're facing the wall

Not he said I'm not facing the wall I'm looking out the window behind you

I turned and for the first time saw a mountain stabbing clear through the clouds and for a moment I turned to Herman who was smiling and loved him and last night 2 am there was Scott

Fat red-head rugby playing Scott
180 pounds
Fat knuckled
Thick legged
Mean

Doggy on all fours muddy socks wet vomiting into the toilet and he and I were going to fight the night before cuz he was making fun of Herman who's THIS close to killing himself and I said Don't be a fuck

Scott said What? Chill out God it was only a joke

And I was THIS close to burning him cuz Herman can't defend himself he's 19 he's had two complete breakdowns so far he's on drugs for his screaming he said When I was a kid I just couldn't stop screaming I couldn't hold onto my emotions like other kids I was different

Scott puked on the floor in the dorm bathroom he said I'm not sorry about trying to get Herman to eat that glue stick

I said You better lay off him

Fuck off he said The retard's here on a computer scholarship and forgets to wipe his ass he shouldn't be here and heaved some more I studied the back of his neck and thought if he were a rabbit I would take him with my teeth and there is sickness everywhere in this dorm nobody flushes you can smell it in the piss on my socks when I go back to my room and in my room we were playing dominoes when Scott stormed in and teased Hey Herman why don't you finish eating this glue stick

I thought I should hurt him scoop his eye in or rip his nose away

And J was there he saw it all and after I kicked Scott outta my room the air hung heavy after Herman left quiet Jason said Something has to be done I hate guys like that I hate white boys like that I hate them We gotta do something I hate it

Looks like the kid the dog and the old man got eaten Jason says and looks up at the ceiling

We listen to the crying and blubbering in the shower and shake our heads

Herman's talking to himself again and I don't think he knows it

So I'll have to move out at the end of the month cuz Scott heard my screaming and the shit is gonna fly when the dorm finds out what we did

Shit

And Herman was THIS close to crying when he said They pennied my door shut and I didn't know who to call This was before I knew you I wish I knew you then

I said How the hell does anyone penny your door shut

They slammed my door shut and three guys pushed it to the frame while someone pushed pennies into the frame to lock the door closed I couldn't open it I knocked on the door for two hours and Scott was laughing in the hallway going You like that retard? You're on the third floor retard why don't you jump!? JUMP!

I wanted Herman to take this take this roar in his head take a black shotgun and light this whole dorm up just grab Scott gut peel and skin him and go just go til he hits the province line and go just go and Dominoes we showed Herman how to play Dominoes for the first time in his life and when I picked up my seven they sounded like bones and Jason told us a baby caribou cries like a cat and I watch Herman cover his smile with his small puppy hand and I think of him this poor first year kid with eyes so close I get a headache if I look into them too long falling in love with all his waitresses and I wonder what it'll be like for him the first time he goes down on the woman who takes him he with such beautiful little songs on the wind his eyes closed as he holds her hands his tongue parting lips and her going I can feel the sky diving between my legs don't stop oh please don't and the roar in his ears as she locks her thighs around him the same roar in his head when he was locked in his room for TWO HOURS Scott booming a basketball off the penny locked door going You like that Retard? You like that?

And Herman can't hear a thing

He can't hear a thing

For once

You listening Herman? Jason asks These are fighting stories from home We're trying to make you strong and Herman nods I tell him there was a moment there when a Slavey Elder stood between his grandchild and a silver tipped grizzly and surrender was never a moment on anyone's lips He had an ax in his hand looking at a silver tipped grizzly with his grandson standing behind him No there was nothing on his lips but COME THE FUCK ON LET'S DO THIS and Herman said Wow neat and Jason asked Did you understand the story Herman? Do you understand what we're trying to give you? And Herman says I think so

I think so

We nod good and pull from the mattress balaclavas

Herman doesn't hold out his hand so we hold it out for him and squeeze I'm taping my knuckles and listening to the Cranes now and man they know that Carnival means the celebration of spinning until the meat flies from your body and

I'm thinking the woman who takes him stands THIS close to Herman before it happens and she says You're always laughing it's the most beautiful sound in the world and he will put his scream away

You have no pupils she says

I do he goes

I have to stand THIS close to you to see them she says

And he can feel the break of her laughter against his face and he feels it she tells him The reason the dogs bark at you when you walk down the street is they know you ate a dog in another life and they can still smell it on your breath and they go crazy biting their own tails and each other's It's your scent not you they hate she says and rises to kiss him and hold him and he closes his eyes and they fall to their knees in secret

I hold my seven dominoes and say Herman here's what we're gonna do we're gonna wear these balaclavas and you and Me and Jason are gonna get Scott and Herman goes Wull are we gonna really beat him up?

I go Yeah we'll roll him

And Herman goes Yeah we'll roll him on the ground

And Jason and I laugh

I called home and told mom about Herman and Scott and I had to stop and open the windows and wipe my eyes and go Everybody in this dorm knows he bullies Herman but nobody does anything

Nobody

They're just as brutal to each other here as they are back home Me and J are on the first floor we can't always watch him and I drop my dominoes and pray Herman'll drop Scott cuz tonight the dogs back home jump in the air spin and try to snap their chains and Me Herman and J played Dominoes and Charles Bukowski AT THE SWEETWATER on disc and I was so disappointed when we finally heard CB's voice and me and J agreed Bukowski should have had the voice of a monster not a boy and Herman asked who is Bukowski? And we said you know Barfly? The movie? The poet? The guy who said *I'm on fire*

> *I'm on fire*
> *like the hands of an acrobat*
> *I'm on fire*

And Jason played his sacred pipe the one he saves for weeping

And tonight we waited in the black no moon shadows Me Herman Jason in balaclavas on the proving ground and Scott staggered from the direction of the campus bar carrying a six pack moving slow

> I'm thinking he works out
> wears a mean face
> loves to ride a soul to pieces
> has a girlfriend—
> Why?

Herman Jason whispers rolling his hood down *There's your silver tipped grizzly Let's tear the night to pieces*

Herman looks at him and I think for a second he's going to wave to Scott

> I run

Jason blows his pipe and Scott stops Who's there?

J blows his pipe again and I let loose my war cry there is a roar in my head and we are wolves

Herman stands in the bushes and watches Scott who's standing tilted looking around I take him throat throw him down while Jason boot staples Scott's nose to his face

> Scott drops
> moaning down

his fat hands trying to plug his gurgling I look at Herman and say Now's your chance! Herman just stands there his balaclava not even down and J looks around and goes Come on man MOVE!! But Herman just stands there I can see his face and I think He's laughing at us he's fuckin' laughing at us I grit my teeth then it hits me he's crying standing there stupid fucking RETARDED—

HEY! Someone calls and we grab Herman back into

the campus forest and he falls and trips HEY! Someone calls
again—CAMPUS SECURITY—STOP!!

We all lay down as there are two of them They run past
and Herman is holding his hands to his face he's crying
sobbing and I'm wet from the grass and Jason has point and
motions We're okay

I whisper Herman Why didn't you do it? We were
holding him man You could have busted him

And Herman holds himself and cries You beat Scott up
You hurt him

I want to go home

I want to

go home I

want to go

home

I hold him this skinned caribou crying like a cat this
little kid who never stopped screaming As he cries into my
chest Jason looks down his bamboo flute broken I

throw

back

my

head

and

roar

Honour Song

there
in the box wrapped in red wool blanket   you there
on top of the flat cedar   you
in the white ash box   you
i sang you home   even though
it was night   i sang   songs   of the Sun
aunt tispit   and me   we drove
you   my mother   home my mother
i sang

out on the Hill   an Eagle lifted off   at dawn
this   i thought of   that day you slipped   you
through the crack of day   your Soul
lifted off   with the power
of a single drop   of water   on the tip
of a Choke   Cherry   leaf

Crooked Nose

To the side of his sway backed bed he rolls.
The light, he fumbles for, its bolting streak

of nightshade glare cannon balls the wall, fireballs
across the pumpkin-pine-board-floor, narrowly

escapes through the squinting crack of venetian
blinds. Another belladonna morning

searching for belt loops, dry socks and cigarettes.
Another body-bag-fog-pressed morning

bleeds his clouded mind to the edge of a
Stewart's coffee cup and grey mystery.

Sediment and fear silt the sink hole of
his offering cauldron travel mug.

And shimmed betwixt his eyelids are well kept
sleepy seeds of anger, they wait, their coiled

chaos like morning datura with its
luscious, closed fluted tongue blossoms fleshy

lips of fragrance unravel sunrise
into a pastoral oblique of greens

that spreads itself as a garden of toads
and slugs, moles and snakes, earthworms and beetles—

each hue cultivating the other, deft
is the hand that tills the syrian rue.

Cleft is the chin that harrows the air with arrogance
the air, the hummingbird swirls its slashing

wings, rises up as did five years ago
again and again, not dead like the sparrow

left under the leathery lobes of bloodroot
but resurrection through the "O" of it all.

The bambilia camouflaged his flaccidity.
Even then, too succulent as fit root

from a distance their opulence everlasting,
but snap: with the pressure of a pastel touch

compassion the colour of fragrant bitter root.
Gravel along the brook reminds him of

the day he found the sparrow stiff
under the canopy of sanguinaria.

There was nothing to let go of but the flutter
of feathery hope a bird no longer needed him

to hold and five years ago it was abrasively
concrete as the thud heard as a car door slammed

but a bird to the windshield to the roadside had fallen
wings, capoeira in the dirt, bathing or dying or

fighting the resurrection that a child's laughter cultivates
until the weight of death itself presses back

the leaves the ancestors cloak their breath with.
No one wants to touch his world

betwixt the wavering gold grasses, fields of it, and
the underneath of his monkshood, and fruitless

may apple where he toys with the idea of light.

Sipping

—for my mother

It was not always bone china, the cup
the saucer, that your long feathered fingered hands wrapped
and chipped as flakes of teeth tunked by the mouth
of a beer bottle: the cup, the saucer, holding
the moisture of an eggshell candling its paper-porcelainess to count
your shadowed maybes on the other side, like in the old days
when kerosene rags haloed your brow of buggy locks.
It only smelt as bad as it was.

No one really believed

the stories of clothing fashioned burlap from sugar—
flour—or potato sacks or that the lamb
really hung itself and its mother bleated for it
for days, her tits festered with grief that you
still added to your tea and stirred with a sterling
spoon with some unknown initial bought with
bottle money at a high-end junk shop because you
could finally do that but no one really believed
the pastoral truth of poverty and trudging for miles
to a colder school than the walk through snow drifts
or the belly-down-face-first sled ride past Springers
not the toboggan ride that broke your leg. You knew
no one had a spirit like yours. But no one
really believed it anymore than the sound of silent
precision of breath and the polyrhythms of chomping bits
and restless hooves while hitching up the team of horses
to the sleigh, buffalo lap blankets and all those brass bells—
gold gilt, brass bells, gold
rimmed your post-menopausal Currier and Ives
tea cups chattering on trays accompanied by different spoons
but still silver and embossed. Com'boss!

Com'boss! And who's boss on the farm
whose soil milked sweat and youth from the backs of boys,
their spines a stack of wafers: no more Canadian jigs.
All compressed into a bale of square cornered hay
and stacks of photo albums and things you wanted to be
when you had enough desire to dream and hope.

Who could have guessed?

No more switchel no more swinging scythe
no more Jimmie Stewart hay rides, no more no
more all in one square cornered hay a kachunking machine
pursed forth a cube of nutrition, ready the black tea,
render the recollections of bitterness that you could not
set down:

Squirrels no longer fascinate me nor do people sitting
in parks or at city bus stops. Joggers
have become common place as the knee pads
on roller bladers, or head phones, cell phones and
micro fiber. But nobody believes me either.

Who'd believe you'd die?

Only the tea
tastes good piping hot from copper kettles,
mine is black, no English twist of milk,
just dark amber that only stark post menopausal bone
china can appreciate with a tinkling curiosity
of what if's and sugar cubes the size of croutons
molasses tan and irregular like brown eggs
brought in from under the hen's ass in a child's hands
cradling the process before bigger hands crack it all
and somewhere between the delicate deliberate bird bites
of fresh bread and raspberry preserves the squeal
of a stuck pig became a seed betwixt your teeth and lard

on the palette your tongue dabbed unconsciously
and repeatedly painting on your retina the
goofiness of horror:
a barking shadow-dog on a canvas tent wall,
the neighbor girl and her baby as they died
in a head on collision. Who'd have guessed it was you
driving behind them and witnessed
the explosive ball of white light a microsecond
prior to impact.
Sitting alone with a cup of tea was almost too much.

Whatever Greek poet said a heifer could be milked
was just damn wrong and no matter how you mixed it
the lamb still hung itself and you ate it.

Suzanne Rancourt

Throwing Stars

At first I thought someone was frying peanut butter
but it was you, really you,
your charred face brittled on the flight mask.
Dog tags you didn't wear any more than seatbelts
tinkled in the cargo hold dangling from the mouths of
luggage
from which clothing exploded, hung, caught up in the
moment,
and wavered like an after shock from the after shock
from the vacuum of the generators
and their brazen light cauterized death into dampness
and late autumn pines.
Heavy frost in Poland Springs—the water froze
from impact too close to home
and the five stars arrived and the m-16s arrived
and the media arrived
and the body bags arrived but you and your buddies
had already gone, flew the coop. Like a Spanish moss
and old olive oil,
your uncontained rancidness leaked through the evergreens.
I never saw your children I never saw your wife I never saw
your mother and father
but I saw the jerk with the camera and his curiosity snatching
memorabilia. Perhaps, he wasn't high tech enough. Perhaps,
he didn't realize all sensitive material had been removed or
maybe we were in his back yard, but really,
it was everyone's backyard.
Howard Hughes only drank Poland Springs' water,
but not that night.
No one drank from the springs that night you busted out of
the sky a screeching fireball,
a pencil point projectile pop-stabbing through
an astronomical poster

you slashed to the Earth, wind sheared white pine tops,
plowed Autumn fields for two miles and burnt.
You were blown out of the vast indifference of space
and attitude,
you just didn't make it home fast enough,
just didn't missile under the live wire soon enough.
Most only knew the half of it and the other half
couldn't give a shit.
Orion fell. We looked for body parts.

When I'm drumming in the park you'd hardly notice
that I knew anything.
If it weren't for my gift of hyper olfactory, I would have
totally forgotten you.
I can smell moth balls for miles, jet fuel for days—sticks
to the roof of my mouth
sends me anaphylactic—I can feel the inside tire blow on a
tractor trailer before I hear it.
A friend had to stop eating meat, can't even be around it,
reminds him of reconnaissance.
Once while jammin'
a drunk fell to the floor trying to dance and drum at the same
time but did neither.
Words soothed him and one night in Saratoga
by the Sulphur spring
in warmer air and damp match sticks waxed our taste buds
while breathing
and the spring pissed in a granite tureen,
the drunk stood still.
In unwavering quiet he listened to words, to poetry, the only
one who understood,
the drunk, had nothing to do with you,
but if he had had a mask
it would have looked like yours.

Suzanne Rancourt

The Viewing

It is because you are still here
that I want to write about you.
Even then, you were not a tall person, your height
reflecting the size of Woodland People.
Round now
but not as a young man pressing your back
into the Desoto's closed truck and the heel
of your booted foot hooked onto the curved, chrome bumper,
hands stuffed the slash pockets of your leather jacket—
Appalachian Jimmie Dean.

I noticed as a child that your hands—
thick and wide as Oak roots and Bear paws—
were like your father's. I noticed
as you handled a wrench, gripped the truck's steering wheel,
or when you moved petrified baby rabbits
from the middle of logging roads. Both of you
rounded, brown and small, crouched
before the rolling dust and grill of a chugging Detroit Diesel.

You swung yourself back into the cab of the truck
hoisting with your Popeye arms—
your feet barely reached the clutch, brakes, accelerator.
I asked, "Why did you do that?"
Between releasing emergency brakes,
extending your 29 inch inseam leg and a slight
grinding of gears, you said, "It ain't easy bein' small."

I didn't think of you as being small.
You're gestures were always so big
like the day you said, "C'mon, Suzie, Herbert's killed the bears."
You pulled you height upright, on two legs, and

136

charged across the lawn and headed next door.
You even took the short cut
through the spruce trees and down the banking to the road
that only us kids and the dogs used.
I skip-trotted to keep up.
My bare, calloused feet and stubbed toes
animated puffs of road side sand.

Herbert lived next door. Already a crowd congregated
to view the bodies displayed side by side belly down
noses parallel.
Herbert sucked his teeth while he talked.
It wasn't as bad as snapping gum but the sounds
were as sharp. He would squint
the eye opposite the corner of the mouth that leered
as the result of his teeth sucking.
As though he had flesh stuck between them.

"C'mon, Suzie, Herbert's killed the bears"
and we went to see for ourselves our relations
rendered waste by bad blood and heat. To see for ourselves
our family: a boar, sow, and two cubs. Both adults weighed in
as the state's largest.
All lived behind our house on the mountain.
You showed me their tracks. How they marked trees, rolled
logs, where they fished.
When they mated they screamed like women
in the hollow. You said they were harmless.
They had their space and we had ours.

Herbert killed the bears and sucked his teeth
and told how easy it was to kill babies,
how the male required more—
heavier trap, shorter chain, more bullets—
Herbert just killed.

You spit a puckering spit that shook the Earth
when it hit just inches from Herbert's feet.
"C'mon, Suzie, we've seen enough."

Respect

Old Yazzie dropped in around three, on foot. I cocked an eye at him that asked what was up, what made him walk three miles down the dirt road, when he knows I pick up Tali from the school bus at 3:45. As usual, he just sat down at my table, no explanations, and waited for coffee. I poured it into two speckled cups and watched him add several heaping spoons of sugar. The milk he added was warm because the gas refrigerator is broken. My thirteen-year-old needs tending, and a widowed archeologist who can't travel to job sites makes a poor living.

Finally, he said in Navajo, "Lotsa people, they been dying."

The dying wasn't news. The Asian flu epidemic was mowing down people on the Rez, even in smart and fancy 1957, and the Indian Health Service wasn't popular.

Yazzie's gnarled-looking fingers kept the cup near his lips, like he wanted the heat close. The winter day was warm, but old age is cold.

"Something's going to happen," he said. "Meier Wash, at the mouth, them rock arts." He looked straight into my eyes for a moment. Both that and him bringing up rock art were unusual. Those petroglyphs are twelve centuries old. The Navajo avoid anything to do with the dead, including their rock art and ruins.

I love rock art, and have spent twenty years on it. I love the Meier Panel especially. The Basketmaker people, centuries before the cliff-dwellers, drew gigantic, human-like figures on the rock, with lines above their heads that suggest to me a spiritual connection with what's above. I believe these figures are shamans, bearers of a knowledge we've lost.

"Maybe you go down to that place 'bout day after tomorrow, go by yourself, have a look. Maybe you tell some people what you see."

I felt a lurch behind my navel. Whatever he wanted me to tell white folks he wouldn't talk to, it was trouble.

Then Yazzie actually explained a little. "This thing," he said, "it's done with songs. The grit, the sandy stuff, it's saved." Then he made a motion of putting something into his mouth.

That was all he would say.

He rode along to meet the bus. When Tali saw him, she took his hand and leaned against him, which is as demonstrative as she gets. He's her great uncle, her maternal grandfather's brother. But in the Navajo way she calls him Grandpa.

"Tali, I can't stay tonight. Got something to do."

She put her arm around her white father and cast sad eyes at her Navajo grandfather. Her eyes said what I already knew. Something was bad wrong.

* * * *

Meier Wash is three round-about hours, across the river and back to it by four-wheel. I left Tali with her relatives in Mythic Valley, so she could play with her cousins.

To avoid the roughest part of the road, I walked the last two miles, and enjoyed stretching my legs. I grew up in this country. Before the war my folks had the trading post at Mythic Valley, fifty miles by dirt road from the nearest supplies. I grew up speaking Navajo to everyone but my parents. Probably was ten years old before I figured out I wasn't Navajo.

Dad used to take me on his pack trips to the great ruins. Some of them, Canyon de Chelly, Betatakin, he discovered those, and knew as much as the scientists he guided back.

The petroglyphs grabbed my imagination and held on. My God, these people chipped art into these huge sandstone walls—CHIPPED it, using antlers or the like. Think of the time, the patience, the determination. Why? What was so important? Why make art instead of planting, gathering food, carrying water, and hunting? Who were they sending a message to? Their descendants? The human race? Themselves? The gods? Why did they care?

One thing was clear to this captivated teenager. For these people, art wasn't leisure, it was survival—if not survival of the body, then the spirit.

When I was eighteen, I went off to the University of Arizona with a keen hunger for knowledge of the ancient ones.

And came back hungry. This is my country. Getting to know it, that's water to the parched earth of my heart.

My wife was born and raised here, Red House Clan, born to Salt Clan. We brought up our children here. Except Tali, they're all gone over now. Reservation life is hard on human beings. For family, I have only Tali left.

For work, I've had the rock art. Where the teenage boy speculated and dreamed, the man learned scientifically and set down hard-won knowledge for everyone. If you were an archeologist, you'd recognize my name, Patrick O. Callahan.

I also helped raise people's awareness about artifacts. When I was a boy, if you found an artifact, you displayed it at home, or, if it was a fine piece, you sold it. Not so much any more. These are treasures, irreplaceable, keys to understanding of a way of life we'll never see again, a way that helps us see what it means to be human. If you take a shard of pottery away, or even a corn cob, much less an entire pot, or a yucca sandal, you are stealing from the legacy of the human race. If you deface rock art, the same. Understand: Even touching rock art damages it, because of the oils in your hand. Though it looks indestructible, it's fragile as desert blossoms.

A few people loot ruins, and make a living at it. I am opposed to capital punishment, except for people who steal or deface Anasazi artifacts.

Now you'll understand why I was dumfounded and

sickened when I saw Meier Panel. The big shaman figures were cut to pieces.

Yazzie.

* * * *

I sat there all day, staring. I am not the sort of man to tell you about rage I felt, or the hot tears I wept.

Not until dark did I start walking back to the car. I made myself stop hurling words at Yazzie—"That art stood for twelve centuries or more... What right did you have...? Those figures had spiritual power... What right...?" Not to mention, "You son of a bitch..."

Step by step along the dirt road in the dark, I forced myself to consider exactly what I'd seen, all of it, what Yazzie had said, and what the meaning was. By the time I picked Tali up, I was making sense of it, and I was calm.

The next day I came back. Probably when Yazzie said tell someone, he meant Dan Stern, the Bureau of Land Management ranger, or Rulon Washburn, the sheriff. Dan would have wrung his hands ineffectually and started the creaky machinery of the Federal Government, which would have led eventually to nasty questions I would refuse to answer.

The sheriff is a blunter sort of fellow, one who divides the world into those who show respect and those who don't. Law-abiding Mormons have respect, the way he sees things, and Indians, hippies, and coloreds don't. Archeologists, along with artists and lovers of wild country, occupy a dubious middle ground. The sheriff would know I'd been tipped off, demand to know who told me, and haul me in on obstruction of justice charges when I wouldn't tell.

Better to let hikers or river-runners report the destruction when they came along in the spring.

The person I took the next day, the person who might need to understand, was Tali.

At first she just gaped, alternately at the rock and at me. I was able to keep a calm look.

Finally I said, "Grandpa Yazzie is responsible for this."

Shock blanched her face.

"He didn't do it himself. A medicine man did, and an assistant. But he asked for the ceremony. He told me this was going to happen."

She couldn't get words out.

"Don't worry, I won't report him."

"You know lots of people have been dying. Your Grandma. Two of your sisters been real sick." (Great aunt and cousins, the way white people figure relations.) "I don't know who else is sick. Looks like Grandpa Yazzie asked for a ceremony. The medicine man came here to get spiritual power."

She was staring off into space now.

"He did a ceremony to shield him, and his assistant, get this near the figures. Grandpa told me it was done with singing."

I pointed at the cuts in the rock, gashes I felt like were in my flesh.

"You could see they were done rhythmically." I looked at my daughter but got nothing. There was nothing to do but go on.

"Look where he struck. Joints. Wrists, ankles, necks, shoulder blades. Nothing else."

"Why?"

So she was following.

"People kidney's get infected. Then they have a lot of joint pain. Then they die."

She nodded. Everyone had heard the stories of how it went.

"Now look on the ground. Grit, lots of it, or sand, where the shards came out. Finger holes where it was picked up. They saved it."

"Why?"

"Two reasons. Your Grandpa told me the patient would eat some, and part was probably used for the sand painting."

She spoke delicately. "Grandpa Yazzie believes in the power of these..."

"And the medicine man did."

"These aren't Navajo."

"Right." I looked at Tali. "Exactly."

"So this, this destroying, it shows..."

"An attitude toward other people's spirit power."

"What attitude?"

"What would you say?"

She thought and whispered, "Respect."

Watersong

Give me back my birthwater
let me be born again
Would somebody first
please dim the bright lights?
All I need is the morningstar
no more rough blankets
put my skin against my Mother's
let her flesh warm me.

Before my birth
let the old women
rub my Mother's belly
with hands that smell of cedar and sage.
No metal stirrups for her legs.

If someone could drum very softly
in time to my Mother's heartsong
with old women and birds singing along.
Let their song instead of the hook
be what induces the waves.
In wombwater I'll be dancing
as they sing me into being.

Please don't sell the Placenta this time
bury it under the red willow tree
and leave a little bundle there for me.

Let the small ocean of life
go into the Earth.
For both of us.
All blessings returned
birth to birth
washing our wombwater
over sweetgrasses
instead of a floor.
All blessings returned.
Life to Life to Life.

Shirley Brozzo

We Have Walked The Same Places

You were there in DC
As I climbed the Lincoln steps.
You were there as I left the bus in the middle
Of Arlington
Surrounded by
Neat rows of white crosses
Standing at attention.
The eternal light flickered
While the somber Marine
Paraded
Before the tomb of the no-longer-unknown
Soldier.
Beggars
Abound on Pennsylvania Avenue
Before the great white house
And just around the corner from
The Disney Store
Hard Rock Café
Planet Hollywood.

You walked there too
Ahead of me
Or behind
Perhaps not even in this lifetime
But another
Yet
I felt your presence there.

I have wandered the length of Bourbon Street
Tasting spicy Cajun food
So foreign to my northern tongue
Marvelled at the cleanliness of the streets

After nights of partying
Shopped the boutiques offering
Fragrant sachets
Sweet treats
Antique crocheted doilies
Crotchless panties.
Nights spent at street parties
With drunken revellers
Jazz musicians
I felt you in the hurricane rain
driven into my skin by the wind
You were there
Ahead or behind
Not in this time
Perhaps
I felt you.

The Rockies beckoned then
And I flew over
Huge circular tracts
Unlike square acres at home.
Snow covered mounts in mid-summer
Shaded in azure fog
While dry heat reigns below
Welcoming after years in the North.
Turquoise Pueblo pottery
Jewellery
Clothes
And eyes.
Drivers are just as crazy as here
Casino glitter
Imported palms on the boulevard.

You were there
Perhaps
Ahead

Behind
Walking.

Beneath eagle's gaze
The lakes are claiming
Lives
Snowmobile riders
Who escape the clutches of the trees
Drinks in flasks
Bottles
Kegs
Modern stills.
Northern Lights fill the skies
Mascots are not struck down
Ceremonies live on near the Rez
National Guard Armory houses spring Pow Wows
Where three dollars gets you fry bread or pasties.

Your footsteps fell there
Behind or above
I felt you this time
Perhaps.

The Voice of the Elders

This time the Elders shall have their voice
And their voices will resound loud and clear
Words of Dine, not Navajo
Words in Lakota, not Sioux
Words from Anishnaabe, not Chippewa

And the children of the Seventh Generation
Will hear and understand
The words of the Elders they hear

This time the Elders shall have their respect
And their wisdom will resound loud and clear
Honour the Elders
Honour the land
Honour thy self

And the children of the Seventh Generation
Will hear and obey
The strong wisdom of the Elders they hear

This time the Elders shall have their say
And their words will not fall on deaf ears
Spoken at home, not from nursing homes
Spoken slowly, not in haste
Spoken from the heart, not in jest

While the children of the Seventh Generation
Listen with heart and soul
To the wisdom words of the Elders

Yes, this time the Elders shall have their voice
And their voices will resound loud and clear

Shirley Brozzo

Tribal words
Honoured words
Spoken words, for all to hear

And the children of the Seventh Generation
Shall recover their roots
The day of the Elders is here!

Mukwa

I just don't know what is going on 'round here. Momma started spending all her time in the city, not even coming home at night to take care of me, so Daddy came and took me to stay with him and Gramma Mel. Daddy said he would have come in off the fishing boat sooner to get me, but he didn't know that Momma wasn't there taking care of me. I just got up in the morning, braided my black hair, ate some Capt'n Crunch and got on the school bus at 7:25. After school I went home and watched Channel 6, ate a bologna sandwich and some commodity cheese and went to bed. I wasn't scared when I was in my own house. All I had to do was look around my little bedroom at the picture of the kodiak bear hanging on the wall, the black bear's tooth that I got from Uncle Alfred, and Gramma Mel's bag made out of a bear's paw. I knew that *Mukwa*, the bear, was there to protect me. My Daddy always told me that I was Bear Clan, and that the bear would always take care of me.

When Momma came back, she was really mad at me for going to Daddy's, but madder still at Daddy for taking me. I could hear them screaming at each other in the living room at Gramma Mel's when they thought that I was asleep. But who could sleep through all that racket?

"Why did you go off and leave her, Kay? She's only nine years old, for Christ sake."

"She's big enough to stay alone for a day or two. We used to at her age, George. Besides, you said you'd be back on Tuesday to get her. I can't even count on you to come in off that fishing boat when you are supposed to."

"The fishing was great. We just couldn't up and leave. You know this is how I make a living for you and her. Al, Erv and I needed this run. Damn it Kay, the season is almost over. This trip determines if we make it or break it."

"It's always that damn boat," Momma screamed. "Those damn fish and your brothers. You're never even home with us any more. Bert is there every night. And he doesn't smell like fish."

"So, it's Bert now. Just like it was Charlie before. And John before that," Daddy retorted.

"Yes," Momma said. "I only came back to get her. Bert said he didn't care if she came. He'll take care of her and me so you can catch your precious fish. She's coming with me tomorrow. We ain't coming back this time."

I lay there crying to myself in the next room. I remembered being with Uncle Charlie. He was tall and skinny like my Daddy and me, and he had black hair, only he wasn't Indian like us. I hated the way he hit Momma, especially when he was drinking. Momma said she didn't like it either, but we stayed with him until she caught him reaching under my nightgown when he was tucking me into bed. I told her he did that lots, but she always told me to shut up. After she saw Uncle Charlie, we moved back home with Daddy. I don't remember anyone name John.

I cried more remembering Charlie and hoping that Bert would not do that too. I didn't want Momma to be hit and I didn't want to be touched, but mostly, I didn't want to leave my Daddy.

By morning, I knew what Momma said was true and not just a dream. Momma was shoving my clothes into pillow cases. I started to cry again.

"Hush, baby. It will be okay. Bert is coming to pick us up in a little while. His house is kind of tiny, but we will all fit for now. You can sleep on the couch. We'll go looking for a new place soon and you can have your own room again. And Bert will be home with us every night. And he doesn't smell like fish."

"I like fish," I said quietly.

"Hush up. We're going," Momma said with a look that I knew meant not to argue with her.

Just as Bert pulled up in his car, Daddy came home to see me. He was carrying a large stuffed animal that I knew had to be for me.

"Here," he said thrusting it at me. "Remember that *Mukwa* will always protect you. Take this bear to bed with you to watch over you. And remember, I love you."

Then he was gone.

Usually I liked going into the city, but this time I did not. I didn't know when I would see my Daddy again. Or Gramma Mel, or Uncle Alfred or Uncle Ervin. I just curled up in the back seat and hugged my bear. I thought I could smell fish on him.

I didn't see any other Indian kids at my new school, but I sure saw lots of brown faces and lots of white faces. Everybody just stared at me; the new kid. I think they laughed at my braids. I didn't have any new friends at all, so after school I went back to Bert's and watched TV. He got Nickelodeon. Momma was never home until just before Bert got home. She'd fly in, her long hair streaming behind her, make us some hamburger casserole, then she and Bert would go out and leave me alone. So I sat and watched TV some more. At least there was more than one channel.

At night I could hear loud people out on the sidewalk and cars zooming up and down the road all night long. I would put my bear's tooth on the table beside the couch where I slept. I'd look at *Mukwa's* picture and put it back under the couch next to my bear paw bag. Then I would hug the stuffed bear my Daddy gave me, pull the blanket over my head, and try to sleep.

Late one night, I woke up to the sound of gun shots. They didn't sound sharp, but I knew what I'd heard. Daddy had taken me out hunting before and we heard Uncle Erv shoot a deer out in the meadow. It kind of sounded like that. I just hugged *Mukwa* tighter, but didn't go back to sleep. I don't think Momma and Bert were even home, cuz nobody came to see if I was okay.

The next day in school, I heard that Jaron's big brother got shot because he owed somebody some money. Back on the Rez, Daddy would have traded something if he didn't have money. I didn't like being in the city. I wanted to go home.

At supper that night Momma and Bert didn't even care that I was scared. They talked about going out to the bar to shoot pool. I begged Momma not to go, but they just left. The traffic on the street sounded louder than usual and people's voices sounded like they were in the same room with me. I tossed and turned on the couch, trying to fight off the noise and go to sleep. I must have fallen asleep for a while, but I jerked awake when there was a loud BANG and the sound of glass breaking. I hugged my teddy bear tighter to me and held my breath. That's when I felt a pain in my side that wouldn't go away, but I was too scared to move.

Much later Momma and Bert came home and found the shattered window. Momma came over to see what had happened. My eyes were wide open. Momma went to pull the bear away from me, but even after I let go, she couldn't pull it away. Then she saw the bullet hole.

At the hospital, the emergency room doctor found that the bullet had just punctured my skin. The bullet was stuck in me. It only bled for a little while. I couldn't go home that night. I had to stay in the hospital. But my bear got to stay with me.

Momma got scared, and went back to Bert's to pack up our things. "We were going back to the Rez," Momma said. She didn't know where we were going to stay, but she knew that we couldn't stay in the city.

Me? I was just glad to be going home. I was going to see my Daddy. And I knew that wherever I was, *Mukwa* would protect me.

How The Beaver Got His Tail

It was spring and the last of the snow had melted. All of the Beavers were crawling out of their houses, welcoming the warmer weather and sunshine. The Beavers began to yawn, and stretch, rubbing the sleep from their eyes and the stiffness from their muscles and bones. They shook their heads and fluffed their bushy tails. Yes, that's right. Beavers used to have fine, bushy tails like the chipmunks and squirrels.

On their first day out of hibernation, they ate and ate. Then they dove into the river, splashing, turning somersaults and playing tag while they took their first bath of the year. Once they felt sufficiently cleaned, the Beavers would climb out of the river and stretch out on the bank to dry. As their tails were drying, the Beavers would nip, paw and preen his or her tail until it was fluffed and dried.

Next on their 'to-do' list was to repair their houses and dams after the long winter. Eagerly, the young Beavers began gnawing down trees. They would chew a little on one side, then chew a little on the other side of the trees until they could get them to fall over. But as you all know, in the spring time a young male's thoughts turn to romance. So it is also with the young male Beavers. Young Bucky Beaver soon began spending more time looking at young Betty Beaver and not paying close attention to what he was supposed to be doing. He would chew and chew as fast as he could to impress her. He would keep on working while the other Beavers took a break. Bucky even offered to share part of his lunch with Betty, but she politely declined and sat with the other girl Beavers. After a short lunch, Bucky went and found an early spring flower to give to Betty, which she tucked behind her ear as she went back to work. After that, Bucky kept glancing her way without watching what was going on around him.

Nearby, Bert Beaver was busy gnawing down a tree. Bucky obviously didn't hear Bert shout "timber!" as his tree began to fall. Bucky just kept admiring Betty. Down, down, down, fell Bert's tree, right across Bucky's tail, squashing it flat.

Bucky began to scream and shout, "Oh my tail. My tail. I can't get it out." He pulled and he strained, but the tree would not budge. Bert and some of the other Beavers came to help pull the tree off Bucky's tail. They tried to roll it off, but it couldn't move because of a large rock behind it. They tried to lift it off, but it was too heavy for them to pick up. Benjamin Beaver offered to cut off Bucky's tail, but all Bucky could do was to cry out in pain.

Finally Betty said, "Why don't you chew the log into smaller pieces and then lift it off Bucky's tail? I'll start."

So several of the Beavers began to chew the log into smaller pieces until they could lift the section off Bucky's tail. Bucky had just about stopped crying from the pain, when he turned around and saw that this smashed tail would not return to its former fluffy self.

He tried to shake it. Nothing happened. He tried to fluff it with his paws. Nothing happened. He dove into the river to get it wet, then returned to the bank. Still nothing happened. Betty felt so bad for Bucky that she gave him a kiss. Again, nothing happened.

Eventually, Bucky and Betty Beaver got together and started a new generation of Beavers, all born with flat tails, as were all the Beavers born, beginning with that generation.

So, if you see Beaver today, you will know how they got their flat tails. You should also learn to pay attention to what is going on around at all times.

Truth and Dare ask Raven "The Big Question"
(and over the rising steam of his coffee... he answers them)

Opening Scene: *Coffee shop (in urban everywhere), present day. Here we find the typical coffee shop, artist types. A little bit on the fringe. The new-age vibes of Enigma filters through the smoke and low din of conversation.*

A heavy glass door slides slowly and gives way to the fleshy brown buck-skinned, Raven. His fingers glint with silver as their tips slide across the surface of the door, smearing it. He checks his pearly whites with a toothpick and sucks out a stuck sesame seed from this morning's bagel and cream cheese. A cotton rainbow shirt—Shakespeare style—balloons around him as his stocky body saunters to the counter.

"Hey Raven, the usual?" All who know him, know him by name and greet him with a big rolling *R*.

"That's right... double latte, hold the milk! You know, my people are lactose intolerant." With a raised eyebrow, he winks with a laugh that rolls off his belly and throughout the crowded coffee shop. The swanky waiter presents the steaming black coffee in an immense ceramic mug, with Raven's name hugging it like a bear, and two packets of whitener.

Raven blows on the hot liquid, cools it a bit and slurps on the caramel, creamed mixture. As usual, he burns his tongue. His dark eyes scan the house for a cozy corner. Everyone here talks the talk but hardly anyone walks the walk. There are murmurs of saving, protecting or protesting whatever species are on the top one million endangered species list. All on the verge of kicking it. Raven shakes his head. No use in sharing in this kind of talk. These guys are all full of it. Words, to them, are just words, with no power. He sidesteps the dead dialogue, moving over to a corner where a hippie couple snuggles in a tie-dyed aura with nappy hair and glazed eyes.

A musky odour of patchouli greets him before the expected and informal, "Dude!" is uttered. They indicate an empty chair and nod him over. Raven turns the chair and straddles it. A man who knows what he likes, like the open wind and riding bareback. He nods his head the way skins greet other skins out on the street. They return the gesture with wide grins and extended hands. Somehow, they know the protocol. Everything is cool and Raven is happy.

Intermission: *The waiter waltzes around the coffee shop floor serenading his customers. Raven joins the waiter for a few rounds before he refills his mug a few more times, just to be on the safe side of his daily caffeine intake. Truth and Dare stumble out for their own fuel-up, returning with a new aura of serenity.*

After another black coffee mixes into Raven's blood stream, his body surrenders to a wave of giggles with a slap of jittery nerves. "...this other time I hitched a ride with a trucker..." Raven and the two hippies, Truth and Dare (obvious nicknames), have all warmed up to each other, now sharing their travel diaries.

"This trucker, as big as, well... me—hehehe," goes Raven's laughter, "picks me up east of Toronto and says he's headed west to the Rockies. He's got another load of cigarettes. Turns out it's his third trip in a month, and he's beginning to think that a change of shipments will be his salvation. He wants no trouble with any Mountie, and man, I don't blame him. So I tells him, 'I'll go with you, I gots my free access card for all points Canadian and American, and if there's trouble... just call for me, Raven.' And, in short, here I am. I haven't left since. And now, Truth and Dare, why you here?"

Their dull eyes mix with the lingering haze. At the same time, "a bad acid trip!" is blurted out between heavy lips.

Smiles wipe across their faces followed by mellow laughter
that's caught in their throat with a re-occurring cough. "Just
kidding, Rave. We're destined to cross this mighty land. This
is our first and last time trip."

Then in hushed voices they admit their ultimate plan,
"We're searching for.... the truth."

"Truth, eh?" Raven ponders through the steam rising
from his coffee. He sighs heavily while motioning out the
window, "It's not out there, dudes. You won't ever find it," he
says, then whispers, "out there."

Dare nudges Truth in the ribs, urging her to ask another
question. Truth rummages through her knapsack and pulls out
some dry tobacco, offering it to Raven.

Raven accepts the gift. He shoves it in his back pocket,
leans back in his chair, becoming stoic. Like those old black
and whites pics of Plains Indians captured by some guy who
then introduced the ideal sad, dying Indian. But this man,
Raven, was far from sad or dying. He just liked that serious
looking Indian bit.

"The truth, Truth and Dare," he says with a slight
chuckle then regains his poise, "is right in front of you. Close
your eyes, take a trip inward, and not down your
innards—hehehe," laughs Raven. *Inwards*. You'll never find
Truth out there when you're right here, in front of me, *but*,"
with a wink, Raven whispers, "you'll always have more fun
out there than in here." With that, Raven knee-slaps both of
them, laughing them awake.

Truth searches Dare's eyes, squinting hard and,
reflecting. She then gets up to leave. Dare shrugs and says,
"Didn't you hear Raven? It's not out there, it's right in front of
you."

Truth turns back and stares right into Dare, "I really
don't like what I saw right in front of me." She swings around
and slips out the door without another word.

"There you have it, Dare, the Truth," Raven says.
"Hehehe," Raven laughs the way he does. "Well, whatcha

waiting for? Ain't gonna chase her?"

Dare shakes his head back and forth for too long and finally stutters, "D-d-do you think I should?"

Raven shakes his head, "Man oh man, enough with all the questions, what do you think? Where is Truth? Is truth inside you, in front of you—or what?!"

Raven picks up his empty mug and sets it on the counter, salutes the waiter, leaving Dare to his stuttering thoughts.

Final Scene: *The waiter in an urban coffee shop turns out the lights and flips the "Open" sign to "Closed," then continues to sweep the floor clean of dust, sand and questions.*

What Happened to Dare?
He still searches for Truth wherever he goes.

What Happened to Truth?
She found it inside of her.

What Happened to Raven?
He's in search of the perfect cup of coffee

...minus the cream.

Black Out.

Chasing the Dragon

Many people don't know that instead of smoking pot, teenagers are smoking heroin. In my seventeen years I have watched three people, who used to be good friends, destroy themselves. I was there when they started to use and I was there when their lives started to unravel. Since then more and more people, my age, have begun to use heroin. That is why I believe that heroin is the next fad.

Teenagers of today aren't looking to be enlightened or inspired like the teenagers of the 60s. I believe this is why many are looking to heroin to get high. A lot of kids have no meaning in their lives and heroin is the perfect escape.

It all starts when they first decide to smoke heroin. At first it's only-once-in-a-while-use. Then once-in-a-while-use turns into everyday use. Soon they are saving all of their money just to get high. After a while they are no longer getting high and they have to smoke more and more. The first time you smoke heroin you get this great high and it's like the chinese proverb about a warrior who spends his life chasing the mythical dragon. If they don't get help or quit soon they eventually graduate to using the needle. Many say they wouldn't because needles scare them, but when you get to this point it's no longer you controlling the drug; it's the drug controlling you. Fear is nothing compared to the need to get high. When times were hard and money was scarce they would get sick. Their stomachs and back would hurt like hell. Sometimes they would get cold/warm chills. And sometimes their knees would shake. Most turned to criminal activity to support their expensive habit. Nothing was too mean or too absurd, as long as they got money to get high. Many didn't believe they would end up the way they did. They never thought they would become addicts. If enough time goes by they eventually hit rock bottom, more than once.

Watching someone you care about hit rock bottom is

very hard, especially watching them do it again and again. It hurts to watch them hurt themselves.

One friend in particular took a lot of energy out of me. You see, this person got stuck in a cycle of self-abuse. He shot, stabbed, robbed, committed home invasions; break and enters, he even stole from friends and family. And he did all of this to get money to buy his heroin. I was there when he got sick. I felt helpless because I couldn't do anything to help him. All I could do was listen to him and try to be a good friend. I saw him on numerous occasions when he was high. His eyes were droopy and glazed. He was slow and his speech was slurred. He would often fall asleep mid-sentence. He often didn't know what was going on. He had recently become an I.V. user. He had overdosed a total of three times. The last time he died. If you are a friend of an addict you should know what you are getting yourself into.

You have to understand that they have a problem and the only thing you can do is be their friend. You cannot force help upon them, they have to want it badly enough to get the help they need. Always let them know how important they are and continue to stand by their side. It's going to be extremely hard and emotionally draining, but I believe everybody deserves someone who is completely crazy about them, mistakes and all. Heroin is an illness which no medicine can cure, and very few escape.

Just Around the Eyes

I sat in the park, children laughing, parents keeping a watchful eye, and that's when I noticed him. With the little bit I saw came a memory, just around the eyes, of someone I've lost. A memory of you. For a moment I thought it was you. He was sitting on a bench, reading the local newspaper, and sipping on a coffee. Standing up quickly, I almost walked over to him, but then reality hit. I sat back down on the grassy hill, my hands trembling as I gasped hard for air. Panting heavily I counted one... two... three... four... five. My breathing returned to normal and the trembling stopped. Calling upon my nerves I walked closer and closer still, until I reached the bench. He looked up at me briefly and smiled. A memory, just around the eyes, of someone I've lost. I got really dizzy and light-headed. Trying not to faint I managed to produce a smile I hoped looked real. I sat down, eyes still fixed on his.

Selina Hanuse

My Mornings

A wobbly ride
Jerked in and out of the morning traffic
Not knowing what to do
Or say
To the knowns
Or the unknowns
Swarms of colours, names and races
Faceless names
Nameless faces
Flock towards that single, wooden building
A cage
A prison
A school?

The Room

The room filled with sorrow; flowers adorned the coffin. People all dressed in black were hugging or crying. Sarah walked and looked around. She saw a lot of her friends, but sat down near the back, by herself. The service seemed to be over and people were saying goodbye one last time. As Sarah wiped her eyes, her mascara marred the whiteness of the tissue. Sarah felt sorrow, although she was unsure why. She didn't know who had died, or why she was there.

As the parade of people passed by the coffin, Sarah saw her family, her mother was thrown over the casket crying.

"Why? Why Sarah? Why my Sarah?" her mother cried.

Sarah stood up and went to walk over to her mother, to tell her that she was okay, but her feet wouldn't cooperate. Angry at her inability to move, Sarah called out to her family. None of them took notice. Not one even looked at her. Sarah started screaming, "Mom! I'm over here. I'm Okay!" Still nothing. Sarah felt this uneasy feeling in the pit of her stomach.

Sarah tried again to move but she still couldn't. Her eyes tried to focus on the pictures that were placed on the coffin, but couldn't. It was a girl, a young girl about her age.

Sarah closed her eyes, and when she opened them she was alone. Sarah stood up and walked slowly towards the coffin. When she got close she closed her eyes and took the last few steps. When she was right in front of the coffin she opened her eyes. She was in shock, it was her...

To be a Child when it Snows

Arms outstretched and spinning round
facing heaven, mouth open wide, she smiled
swallowed a mouthful of diamonds as they
fell
from the sky.

Twelfth Christmas

I awoke to the smell of pine trees and something baking. The sun wasn't out yet, but it was warm nonetheless. I jumped out of bed and ran all the way downstairs. The holiday tree was dressed to the nines. Underneath lay treasures galore. My eyes widened as I saw the large red and white package.

I got so excited I ran and began the search for a name. When I finally found the identification tag, I saw my name printed in bright, gold letters. It was my twelfth Christmas, and the best one ever. I unwrapped the huge gift hungrily, clawing at the wrapping paper.

It seems so long ago. I can't even remember what was in the box, but maybe that wasn't what was important. What was important was, after six years, I can still remember that feeling as I unwrapped that box.

Horror Hill

PART I

"Why do we have to go to Hollow Hill for Halloween?" I asked my mom.

"Because that's where I grew up and I want you and your brother to see where I used to live when I was a little girl." She answered that same question for ten minutes.

"I want to go Mom!" said my stupid little brother Isaac.

"See, even your brother wants to go. Now I know you wanted to go out with your friends for Halloween, but you're just going to have to come whether you like it or not, and that is final," my mom yelled at me.

"It's not fair! I'm thirteen years old, I should be able to decide for myself!" I yelled back at my mom. I stomped out of the kitchen and upstairs to my room. I could hear my mom calling my name, but I kept walking.

Before I get on with my story, I'm going to tell you a bit about my family and me. My name is Kelly Kerfowski and I'm thirteen. Isaac is ten. My mom is thirty-five and my dad died in a car accident two years ago.

Enough about me, let's get on with the story. Well, as you know I didn't want to go to Hollow Hill because I was supposed to go trick-or-treating with my two best friends, Lisa and Rose. That night I did three-way-calling with them. This was our conversation:

Me: Guess what?
Rose and Lisa: What?
Me: I have to go to Hollow Hill this weekend, and Halloween is this weekend.
Rose: That means you can't come trick-or-treating with us.
Lisa: That totally sucks. Did your mom make you?
Me: She sure did. Do you know anything about Hollow

Hill? ... anyone?

Lisa: I heard some people call it Horror Hill.

Rose: Why?

Lisa: Because people were murdered there. Also there are ghosts that come out on Halloween to get revenge on their murderers or just to haunt someone.

Me: Is this true, because that's where my dad died.

Rose: Probably.

Me: Wait, I got to hang up. My mom is coming.

Click.

"Kelly pack up!" my mom yelled.

"OKAY!"

The next day was really cloudy. It was Saturday. My mom was yelling at me because I got up late. She took my suitcase and threw it in the backseat.

"Get in the car."

"I'm not sitting in the backseat!"

"Yes you are."

"No, I'm not! I'm sitting in the front where I always sit."

"Isaac is sitting in the front! DO I MAKE MYSELF CLEAR?" and then she slapped me across the face.

"Yes ma'am." *I hate her,* I thought, *I really hate her.*

The drive to Hollow Hill was about two hours from Denver. It was long and boring. My brother kept playing his stupid music all the way there.

When we finally got to Hollow Hill, my mom calmed down and was singing and smiling. *Good, she's in a good mood,* I thought. We pulled in at Grandma's house, and she was waiting outside with Grandpa in a wheelchair.

"Come here my little lollipop." With those words she pointed to Isaac.

"Grandma! Grandpa! Isaac ran over to them and hugged and kissed them. After he was done it was my turn. Oh no, I'm too old to be kissed! I thought.

Dinner that night was terrifying, everyone was quiet. I

169

wanted to start a conversation, so I asked Isaac what he was going to be for Halloween. He said he was going to be a pirate. I shouldn't have said anything because now I got myself into another argument with my mom.

"Kelly, you're going to take your brother out for Halloween, okay?" Mom asked me.

"Of course not. I'm not going with anyone. I'm going by myself." I answered her.

"You're going to take him out and I don't want any arguments." she told me.

"Grandma, may I please be excused to my room?" I asked Grandma.

"Where to, Kelly Teddy?" *I hate it when she calls me that.*

"To my room. Oh, and next time I ask you something, I'm much too old to be called a silly and childish nickname, okay?"

"You may go and I'll try not to," she told me.

That night before I went to bed I read a ghost story to get myself in the mood for Halloween. I fell asleep a few minutes later. A while later I woke up and my curtains were blowing in the wind as if something had come in my window. I went to the window and closed it. I wasn't afraid because I thought it was my brother playing a pre-Halloween prank. Before I went back to sleep, I murmured, I hate this town.

The next day which was Halloween, was really boring. I mean super boring. I was actually excited to take Isaac out for Halloween. I took him all over this little town. It only took us two hours to do the whole town. He was disappointed when we came home because he didn't get as much candy as he did in Denver. I was happy because I'd finally get something to munch on. But, when we got home no one was home. There was no note saying where everyone was. I told Isaac to go to the neighbours house and stay there until everyone got home. I wanted to explore this town's cemetery and see if you could really see ghosts.

When I got to the cemetery there was a full moon. It was Sunday, so all the ghosts would be in the cemetery. My dad was buried here and I wanted to talk to him because I really missed him. Once in the cemetery, I got the strangest feeling that someone or something was following me. I kept looking behind me, but every time I looked it would disappear. Suddenly, this big black figure came out of nowhere and grabbed me. I let out a little scream. Then all these other ghostly figures came at me.

"No children in the graveyard after midnight," said a strange voice.

"I don't live around here! What are you going to do to me?" I yelled.

"EAT EAT EAT EAT EAT EAT!" chanted the zombies.

I screamed again. They started grabbing me all over the place, and biting me and I kept screaming louder and louder until I felt like this was it. This was my last moment on this horrible earth. I had flashbacks from when I was born to my last argument with Mom. *Wait, no,* I thought, *I'm going to get out of this mess whether they like it or not.*

I kicked a zombie's head off and another's finger and another's leg and another's arm, anything until they were all off me. I took a deep breath and started running away to my father's grave. I looked back and the zombies were reconnecting their body parts. I wasn't halfway to the grave when I remembered the pain in my body from the zombies and fell to the ground. Suddenly more zombies came out of nowhere and I jumped up from the ground and started running away again. A zombie grabbed my foot and I kept on running until more of them jumped on me chanting, "No Escape. No Escape."

I finally fell to the ground giving me hope. I knew it was over. I was so close to my dad's grave that I called his name, who knows how many times. They were close to finishing eating my left leg, when suddenly a big white light shone from my dad's grave. My dad appeared and all the zombies scrambled back to their graves. I don't know why, but I started crying when I saw my dad.

"Kelly, you must go home," he told me.

"But why, Dad? I want to talk to you. Why did the zombies run away when they saw you?"

"You ask too many questions. I will tell you everything when it is time. You must go home because someone you love very dearly will soon be gone."

"But I love you Daddy. I want you to come home."

"I can't. I love you too, but you have to go home now."

I wanted to see if I could hug him, so I went over to him. He knew what I wanted so he came down to the ground. We hugged. It felt like nothing I ever felt before. I didn't want it to end and I knew he felt the same way, but it had to end.

"Go home now. I love you. Goodbye." I took one last good look at him and I saw tears roll down his transparent cheeks. I never knew ghosts could cry. I was crying since the beginning. I looked down at my leg, nothing was wrong with it, for he had healed it. He slowly disappeared in the tombstone. I turned and walked away, to home.

When I got home, Grandma and Mom were crying.

"Where's Isaac?" I asked.

"Sleeping," Mom managed to say through tears.

"Where is Grandpa and why are you crying?" I asked.

"We have to talk to you Kelly," Grandma said and then looked at Mom.

I knew what Mom would say, that Grandpa was dead.

"Not long after you took Isaac out for Halloween... Grandpa had a heart attack and we rushed him to the hospital, but we were too late." Mom started crying even more.

Grandma hugged her and opened her arms for me to come to them. I went. I started crying too. I was happy, but I was sad.

I looked out the window and saw a herd of zombies coming. *Oh no!* I thought.

The end for now.

"So Yous Wount Be Put Away"

AN EXPRESSION FROM MY MOTHER, STILL LOUD AND CLEAR IN MY EARS

My Mother spoke these words to her children almost every week. My Mom's Mohawk name was She Picks Flowers. Whenever a situation arose where she wanted me to feel fortunate in life. She would express herself as best of what she felt she could. I was thirteen when I found out vital information about her life and her actual survival. I was thirty years old when I finally really knew and understood about her cries for sanity, and why I was beaten and abused. This was her means of expressing her white fears including the need to be safe and her need to be loved. She would never really speak about the loss of her Identity, her Name and her Spirit. And I feel and see this haunting, this depth of pain and frustration shadowing, covering and protruding over my family. This breeding into generations yet to come. All Mom would say is, "Just be good, so yous wount be put away, like I was."

1927. My Mom was institutionalized at the age of eight years young, along with her younger sister and two younger brothers. She was sold to the Anglican Church by her father for two horses and a wagon at Tyendinaga Reserve. On which he took all four to Belleville to the train and shipped them to Sault Saint Marie, Ontario. There they all resided in a concentration camp called Singwauk for some ten years. Mom did mention her strength and need for survival was attributed to longing and waiting to go back home to see her mother again. My mother only expressed bitterness and shame. Sorrow and depression and the need for being unloved and abused. And now all these expressions all breed and haunt my family. We all sit and hide in the red shadows of white fear in this untold yellow slimy valley of this so called politics and church.

She Picks Flowers has left for her Peace and journey to the Strawberry Fields forever. This happened just two years ago this fall. And I know inside my heart this is where she is safe and feels loved. She waits for me to join her. There we can be in Harmony of Life and pick strawberry forever. I will see you soon dear Mother. I can wrap my arms around you and feel the love we couldn't share. But, thank you for the best of things which you could share and your biggest fear "so yous wount be put away."

I now have four children and eleven grandchildren. I started my own branch of the Mohawk Nation. And we still hide under the white quilt of fear and walk in these blood red shadows. "So WE wount be put away."

Our love and survival is hidden behind these scared white fears and deep, deep pain. I have carried now for some sixty years, the anguish and suffering of pain of my Mom.

I walk strong with my white quilt of shame, my disguise. I walk strong with frustration stepping softly in my moccasins. This respected Mohawk Elder, Strong Warrior Woman of the Wolf Clan of the Mohawk Nation, today in this year 2000, each day left for me allows me the opportunity to write and express my spirit and myself.

Each Day teaches me about Peace and the freedom of respect. And I will not, no I wount be put away. Each Day prepares me for the walk up the Milky Way to Our Strawberry Fields, where All Women can pick in strawberries forever.

See you soon Mom.   Kayenderes

Marguerite

Her name was Marguerite. She was my grandmother, whose essence was only captured twice by opportunity. One opportunity sits collecting dust within the confines of my parents' china cabinet. Framed on a bone-white china dinner plate is a photograph of a plain woman with small, dark eyes. Her straight, black hair fashioned with a centre part that rarely deviated from its intention, falls in uneven edges to just above her shoulders. I see in her features traces of noble, quiet strength that came to her through the bloodline of a Cree and French descent. Standing to her right is the one I knew as 'Grandpa,' a surly Englishman who rarely spoke. My distant living memory of him is around the time of my thirteenth birthday, as he is given a military burial in honour of his service to God and Country during WWI. Perhaps there is no irony in the second image of my grandmother that remains etched in my consciousness.

It is the picture of her funeral that commands my retrospective ascent into her legacy first. I believe that my father is thirteen years old, and he is standing beside her open casket. Within the crowd gathered around him are a few faces I recognize as his brothers and sisters, all rendered in a design of grief, coloured black and white. Others that are present outline something of my father's expression, tones of confusion and disbelief. I think that I had seen the picture in one of my Auntie's photo albums. I can't be sure, it was a years ago. What haunts me now is not tragic, woeful loss, but the need to dedicate and restore honour for the gift she has given me.

What is this gift? I believe it is ancestral legacy, granted in the reflection of a memory about a woman no one speaks of because her earthly record is so far from the life they were forced to live without her? There has become a persistent longing to know about her, in greater detail that would lead me to understanding some of my heritage, that for so long was treated with silence and secrecy. But what is it that I know about her already?

"She died in the hospital, that's why Dad hated the church." As I listened intently to the discussion taking place, my child ears peaking with curiosity, one of the adults followed with the explanation that the nuns, who were responsible for my grandmothers' care and delivery of her infant, failed in their duties. She would fatally hemorrhage, and at the age of thirty-nine, being survived by a husband twenty-two years her senior and ten children, leave the world behind to return to the loving arms of the Creator.

As an adult, I became privy to knowledge that neither shocked nor stunned me. "She came for help once, with the kids, because she was being beaten by the old man." Life treated her harshly, I have no doubt. It is part of my collective intuition. That there would be anything less than honour and respect for all deeds done with nothing to be ashamed of is what most of us deserve. This is far from the truth for some, perhaps most. I ask myself, how the disclosure of a less than perfect family history serves the memory of Marguerite? I can't be certain of its' effect. Some of my people would be wounded and protest exaggeration on the part of me, the writer. The disclosure could create the opening of older, much deeper wounds than have been tended to, and succumbed to healing such as healing becomes when it is so far from the present. Is this what I owe my grandmother? Acknowledgement of her pain, or was hers of so little consequence because she would leave to be with the Creator before anyone would have a chance to record her legacy.

My point of reference into her nature takes me to the picture in the china cabinet. Mystery surrounds and permeates her image within the confines of my imagination. Herein lies my fascination and inherent difficulties with not having known her, even for a single moment. I can only realize conjectures of the soul and spirit that entertained an identity and lifestyle within the confines of flesh and bone. More practical souls in my world argue that a photograph is not meant to capture personality, desires, wishes for the prying eyes of a curious granddaughter. Nor was it the intention of the photographic sitting to be more than a moment captured for posterity of a family in the mid 1920s to be held, cherished and passed on, to be nothing more than a staple in a bulging, yellowing photo album. Is there a need for more unanswerable questions? My subconscious suggests to take in the images, placing them in my own synaptic recesses as people I have come from and be satisfied with that. So what of Marguerite?

The question remains to be dealt a fair and satisfactory answer, not just for my own selfish, self-absorbed benefit, or is it? I have Aboriginal roots but I am a fair-skinned, freckled-faced, blue-eyed woman whose claim to that heritage is through Marguerite. I have a Métis card, but feel inadequate and subject to ridicule by my Aboriginal brothers and sisters if I use it. Although I have not encountered such treatment, I step cautiously into the arena of a community and culture I want to know more about.

Not so long ago, I was forced, through stress-induced vulnerability, into the world of spirituality, mysticism and holistic practices. I would discover the purpose of my existence on this Earthly plane was to teach the things that I was here to learn. As difficult as I found this to concede, I allowed my Spirit to navigate my direction and so began my humble beginnings as a newly found seeker of my own reality. In doing so, I was obligated to come to an agreement with the past, present and future elements that have created my dharma. These elements are ascribed through an affinity and desire to understand my Aboriginal ancestors.

Through Spirit, I heard a sound from within that is the voice of the ancestors to whom we are indebted. I learned from a quiet, diminutive Shaman about the significance of tobacco as a sacred offering to the Spirit World. Hungry for more answers to my questions about the Spirits and his experiences,

I bombarded him with questions, which, with infinite patience and grace, he answered only the ones he felt I was intended to know. I left the experience feeling hungrier. I decided to learn more, but circumstances would have me follow a journey more pragmatic and grounded in the world I have lived in for so long. I gravitated towards the picture in the china cabinet, focussing on Marguerite.

I started a painting for her. Through the channel of Spirit, I began to create an image of her as if she were singing to my heart centre. I depicted her with eyes closed imagining away brutal fists and crushing blows. Her modest, worn spirit being was instead to be caressed by gentle strokes and loving touches cascading from Heaven. With deliberate and candid passion I let the brush find the right stroke to discover her meaning. I stop to meditate on her animal spirit and from her own heart centre, unfolds the symbol of a bird in pale brown hues. What emerges from that is the form of an infant yet to be born and would bring with her, ancient and compelling knowledge. The evolution of the process is catharsis as I purged context, archetypes and ancestral legacy. All of this created to honour Marguerite.

Marguerite did exist on this plane. Had she lived, she would be opening a new century with a life nearly ninety-seven years long. I want to believe that had she lived, I would know the details of my heritage. These details would have been filled in with coloured narratives of history, events and the characters who supported the legacy. I would have had a much richer, fuller black and white photograph of my grandmother. My dedication to her would have been truer, perhaps with less whimsy and romance, as I tried to capture her essence on canvas and within these words.

Even though there are two people being represented in a photograph, amateurishly trimmed and pasted to a simple, white dinner plate, I feel the need to focus on the woman I never knew as grandmother. What could she have taught me about having Aboriginal ancestry? Perhaps it was her way, any dreams, wishes or desires to be left unspoken. My father never speaks of her, nor have I ever asked. I sense there is so very much pain. It would be the last thing left to honour. Silently, and in my heart centre, through Spirit, I pray that grace and honour be restored to Marguerite, such a beautiful name.

Dan Ennis

The Story of My Childhood Journey In The White Wilderness

Once a beautiful Aboriginal child was born, a child full of light, life, love and peace. He was innocent and open, full of passion and joy. He saw light and happiness in everything, and he knew with his heart that was connected to all he saw. He knew instinctively that he was related to all of Creation and that he was part of his Earth Mother, a connection that would last a lifetime. This child of light also knew in his heart that this connection needed to be nurtured, protected, respected and observed through ceremonies for a lifetime.

But, as this child grew older, things began to change as outside forces bombarded him. By the age of twelve, most of the light, love, peace and sense of connection had been replaced by fear, isolation, anger and hate. He was becoming an adult who forgot about his heart and only used his brain. This meant he also forgot intuition and the sacred, spiritual aspects of his being. The spiritual light grew dim. The sacred part of his being began to shrink and harden. By the time he was an adult, this sacred part was so small and lifeless, it seemed to be nonexistent. So he lived the next fifteen years like other adults who had lost their light, and he filled the void with alcohol or drugs so the pain of his loss would be dulled.

Fortunately for him, there were still people in his life who retained their connection and light-energy. No matter how much he tried to ignore or forget them, these people were there to be his teachers. By now, his father had passed on, but his mother was still doing what she could to keep her son open to this light-energy. Then, the woman who would eventually become his wife was placed in his path to help him open again to the light.

After marriage, the man who had lost his light was blessed with two sons. These children were as he had once been, beautiful children full of light-energy and love. But nothing could return him to those early days of light. Nothing,

180

until he turned forty-three years of age. At this time he was forced to undergo surgery. It was in the recovery room after this operation that the radiant light-energy he had stuffed down for all those years and covered with hurt and anger finally managed to surface. It dug its way out of the solid dark, polluted mass of anger, fear, hate, resentment, rage, ego, bitterness, helplessness, hopelessness and loneliness—all that toxic garbage that had accumulated through the years. The light surfaced to pay him a visit. It came in the form of a miniature image of himself.

This tiny image came out while the man slipped in and out of consciousness after the surgery. The tiny person came out of his left eye and looked around. This small person did not like what he saw and immediately went back inside through the same place where he had earlier emerged. Later that same day, the man got very nauseous. He called for a nurse and asked for a bed pan. In a short time, he began to vomit. He vomited for a long time; it felt like hours. Then, he noticed that the vomit was black in colour, shiny and almost solid in density. There appeared to be gallons of it!

Unfortunately, the man did not immediately recognize that the black vomit represented his negative, hate-filled and fear-filled life. He did not connect with that other self. He was only glad to put the fearful experience behind him.

The man did not recognize that his thirty years of wandering in the wilderness of white civilization had left him feeling lost, confused and fearful. It had taken away his identity and he no longer knew who he was. He did not recognize that most of his health problems, drinking problems, marriage problems, parenting problems, and spiritual problems, all stemmed from this loss of light-energy and his connectedness to Earth Mother and all her creatures. For thirty years he had been trying to make himself into something he could never become: a white person. He did not recognize what his tiny visitor and all that black vomit were trying to show him. He could not understand that he was being urged to let go of all that heavy bag of garbage he had carried for so long, all the hate, all the fear, all the rage and all the false male ego that prevented his healing. That meant letting go of the past.

It was some time after the experience in that recovery that the man began to look seriously at the traditional teachings and sacred practices of his people. He began to actively seek out the Medicine Elders through books and films, and whenever possible, in person. He began attending pow wows, traditional gatherings, spiritual gatherings and spiritual ceremonies. He began to make connections with all of his personal, marital, family and emotional dysfunctions. He began to see the self-condemnation, lack of self-esteem and loss of self-respect that had overtaken him in his attempt to become someone he could never become. He could never become white.

Slowly, he began to feel in his heart again. He began to believe he could have the strength to let go of the past and this heavy burden he had been carrying for so long. Being a modern male, having done time in gangs, in the military and as a competitor is sports teams, he had been conditioned into thinking of himself as a tough man. That meant he could show no emotion if he were to be strong and fearless. But, he soon began to realize that this macho image only hid a very weak, fear-filled human being. It was with this realization that the man began to reconnect with the beautiful light-filled child from so long ago. He began to recognize his sacred connection the Sacred Earth Mother, all the grandmothers, the aunts, the mates, the sisters, the daughters, and the granddaughters who are the life givers.

Through the Medicine Elders' traditional teachings, and the sacred ceremonies such as the Sweat Lodge Ceremony, he began to heal and experience tremendous spiritual growth. That beautiful, spiritual child who had been born full of light forty years before had begun his journey back to the light. Like so many children who arrive in this world as creatures of light and love and peace, a gift from the Creator, this man had lost his true self through the journey to adulthood. Man-made religion, laws, and social norms had robbed him of those sacred birth gifts.

In 1993, Creator blessed this man and his wife with another very sacred gift. A new spiritual teacher arrived in the form of a grandson, and immediately he began to teach the sacred ways of the ancestors. The man who had been unable to hear the teachings that had come from his two sons sent by the Creator so long before, was now able to pay close attention to this new teacher.

Today, it is still difficult for the man who had once lost his light-energy to hear all this tiny teacher has to bring to him. Much damage was done to this man by heartless adults, authorities and institutions in the white wilderness and sometimes his hearing is still impaired. But his desire for spiritual growth continues and his spirit continues to heal.

When the grandson was about three years old, the man experienced a vision of him during a Sweat Lodge Ceremony. He saw the image of two human beings. One was small and one much larger and they were walking away from the man hand in hand. The image evoked feelings of love, safety, security and protection. The man immediately assumed that the larger adult male represented himself and the smaller one represented his grandson. But he was wrong.

At another Sweat Lodge Ceremony, he had a similar vision. This time the grandson made it unmistakably clear that the larger human being was not the man but rather the grandchild. The small child in the vision was instead his grandfather, this man on his healing journey. Once again, feelings of safety, security and protection overwhelmed the man. He was taken back in thought to the times he had walked hand in hand with those people who had cared most for him as a child: his grandmother, his grandfather, his mom and his dad. He felt the security and joy of feeling the hand of all those persons who believed him to be a special gift. Walking with them and listening to their voices, had fed that light-energy. He radiated in their presence. All of these feelings flooded the man as he experienced this vision in theSweat Lodge.

The grandson made it very clear that the man was, indeed, the child who needed guidance and protection. The man needed to feel the security of a loving hand in order to complete his healing journey. The man began to recognize, acknowledge and accept this child as his spirit teacher. He knew this child was a sacred gift with those special powers given by Creator. This knowledge filled the man's heart and his spiritual growth began to increase at a much more rapid pace than he had ever experienced.

Now, with his spirit teacher holding his hand and guiding him, the man could see and feel his spiritual growth as he accepted that this healing, changing and growing would be a lifelong endeavour. And, even though the man could feel the light again in his heart, he was also sadly aware that much had been lost. He would never be the same radiant, light-filled, love-filled teacher who had thrived before all the educators, religious people, bureaucrats, politicians and other dysfunctional people had beaten and lied and ignored him as they systematically extinguished that light so he could conform to life 'in the real world.' Not during this earthwalk, at least.

But, today that man knows who he is and where he is going. He is no longer a small Aboriginal child lost in a white wilderness. Today, he has learned to love who he is and to let go of fear. He holds to the assurance that his spirit teacher is with him, and every day he gives thanks that the long, lonely, spirit-breaking journey in the wilderness of white civilization is finally over. Each day he meditates and asks for help from the powers of the Six Directions that he might remain on the healing path of life, the red road, and continue to grow spiritually moment by moment.

AUTHOR
NOTES

Carol Snow Moon Bachofner

Carol Snow Moon Bachofner, Abenaki, writes a regular column in
Fresh Ink, a publication of California Writers Club. She is a mentor
and caucus member of Wordcraft Circle of Native Writers &
Storytellers. In 1999 Carol was named Wordcrafter of the Year.
Recent publications include E. L. F. Eclectic Literary Forum,
Gatherings IX, My Home As I Remember and the Dan Rive
Anthology 2000. Carol teaches poetry workshops online and in the
conference setting.

Win Blevins

Win Blevins' Welsh-Cherokee ancestors came west to Indian
Territory on the Trail of Tears. He now lives in the Four Corners, on
the edge of the Navajo Reservation. He's the author of nine novels,
four books of non-fiction and thousands of articles. His novelistic
biography of Crazy Horse, Stone Song, won the Spur Award and the
Mountain and Plains Booksellers Award for fiction in 1995.

Shirley Brozzo

I am Keweenaw Bay Anishnaabe currently living in Marquette, MI.
I am employed at Northern Michigan University as the Coordinator
of the Gateway Academic Program, a support program for students
of colour on campus. I also teach in the Native American Studies
Department. For the past two years I have been on the Executive
Board of Wordcraft Circle, and was one of the two founding student
members in 1992.

James Colbert

My fiction in various forms has been translated into seven languages
and distributed in over forty countries. Stories from this same
thematic collection-in-progress have been chosen as a finalist for
STORY'S Carson McCullers Prize and for a Greensboro Award I
have been published in Flyaway and the Cimarron Review. I have
also been an enlisted Marine, an air controller, a cabinetmaker, a
bartender, a police officer; presently, I am an assistant professor of
English at the University of New Mexico. I am, too, an enrolled
member of the Chickasaw Nation.

D. Lynn Daniels

My name is D. Lynn Daniels. My journey into the art and writing world has been slow and wrought with insecurity and fear. It was always suggested that such a pursuit was nonsense (there is no money in it!), and the need to get a real job was the only solution to making a living. I believe that by giving voice to my own needs, I may actually be able to live my life according to Spirit. This is my vocation and I will persevere until I can no longer hear that voice. I am becoming an emerging artist and freelance writer living in Edmonton. I am not being a hypocrite by having a day job as Managing Editor and publisher for a local publishing firm, as well as my own business, Angel Studios & Workshop. Am I?

Dawn Dumont

Dawn Dumont, a Cree woman from the Okanese First Nation in Saskatchewan, is currently living in Toronto. She is a writer of short stories, screenplays, plays and poems. Poetry remains her first love and her primary medium of expression. She believes that poetry is a special language that you can hear only when you listen with your heart.

William George

William George is from the Burrard Indian Reserve in North Vancouver, BC. His poem, "Moment Will Pass" is published in *A Shade of Spring: An Anthology of New Native Writers* by 7th Generation Books and his poem "Blanket Needs" is published in Let The Drums Be Your Heart, edited by Joel Maki, published by Douglas & MacIntyre. William also has work published in previous volumes of Gatherings. He is currently studying Writing at the University of Victoria.

Linda LeGarde Grover

I am a member of the Bois Forte Band of the Minnesota Chippewa Tribe, and have published poetry in several collections and magazines, including the Eclectic Literary Forum, The Roaring Muse, and the recently published My Home as I Remember by Native Women in the Arts. I have also co-authored a set of social studies books for elementary level students about Anishnaabe family life in the early 20th century. I teach in the American Indian Studies and Education departments at the University of Minnesota, Duluth.

Selina Hanuse

Selina Ruby May Hanuse, age seventeen, was registered through her mother's line with the Cape Mudge band near Campbell River, BC. Her father was Nimkish. Selina is probably best known to the public for her role as a child actor on the CBC TV show "North of 60". She was a student at Total Education school in Vancouver and was six months away from her graduation when she was struck and killed in a crosswalk Jan. 3, 2000, by a speeding car.

Jane Inyallie

Jane Inyallie is Tse'khene from McLeod Lake and a graduate of the En'owkin School of Writing. She lives in Vanderhoof, BC, and works at Vanderhoof Alcohol & Drug Services. She spends summers on the trails of BC hiking with her partner, three dogs, goat and donkey. They have a beautiful little grandson named Craig.

Kayenderes

Elder Kayenderes has been handed her traditional Mohawk teachings by her ancestors at Six Nations Reservation from the time she was young. Her true teachers of life are the environment, her Elders, her tradition, Mohawk culture and the Creator. As a political activist, she was involved in three armed confrontations. Some of her professional training is from the University of California at Davis. She has travelled and lectured internationally and nationally since 1975. Her accomplishments include work in areas of Paranormal psychology, Residential abuse, Art and Music. Her work with Native Peoples include the US, Canada and Australia. She recently returned from a working camp in Germany and lectured at a Women's conference on Native Traditional and Self Healing for Survival. She states, "At this age, I want to be emerging like a Yellow Moccasin Orchid. I want my art and my writings to live in the heart of all peoples. I want to be understood and respected and heard with my truth. *And I wount be put away.*"

Leanne Flett Kruger

Leanne Flett Kruger is a mixed-blood Anishinaabe/Cree/Métis. She is presently completing her final year at the En'owkin International School of Writing, in their First Nations Creative Writing Certifcate Program.

Vera Manuel

Vera Manuel is Secwepemc-Ktunaxa from the Interior of British Columbia. She is a storyteller, poet, playwright and the founder of Storyteller Productions which produces creative material addressing issues of First Nations communities. Vera travels extensively across Canada and the U.S. facilitating processess of healing from cultural oppression and multigenerational trauma and grief. Vera has just completed a new play titled "Every Warriors Song."

Laura A. Marsden

Laura A. Marsden is an Anishinaabe writer and artist from the Scugog and Rama Reserves in Ontario. During her lifetime, Ms. Marsden has developed a style which is culturally explicit, translative of traditional and contemporary mediums. "The art of writing legends is the scholar's ability to capture the dream, provide accurate documentation, and acknowledgement of the Elders."

MariJo Moore

MariJo Moore (Cherokee) is the author of Spirit Voices of Bones, Crow Quotes, Tree Quotes, Desert Quotes, Red Woman With Backward Eyes and editor of Feeding The Ancient Fires: A Collection of Writings by North Carolina American Indians. In 1998, she was chosen as NC's Distinguished Woman of the Year in the Arts. She is founder of Red Woman Creations, INC., a national non-profit organization (based in Western NC) whose mission is to promote and preserve American Indian cultures and languages though the humanities with the focus on American Indian youth.

Vanessa Nelson

I was born on October 28, 1986. I have two brothers and no sisters. I am the youngest. I am Mohawk and French. I speak English and a bit of French. I like reading.

Margaret Orr

Margaret Orr is a James Bay Cree from Northern Quebec. Her Cree, Inuit, Scottish and French ancestry has lead her to many places and experiences. Having spent her childhood on Fort George Island and the surrounding territory, Margaret learned the importance of nature from her observations and from the teachings of her Elders. Later, she went on to college and achieved a Fine Arts degree at CEGEP. Then on to Saskatchewan where she graduated with a BFA in Indian Arts at SIFC. That same year, 1998, Margaret travelled with her three children to Penticton, BC, and studied Creative Writing at the En'owkin Centre for two years.

Eric A. Ostrowidzki

I am a member of the Abenakis Nation located on the Odanak Reserve in Quebec. I have a Bachelors and Masters of Arts in English Literature from McGill University. Presently, I am finishing up my doctoral degree in Literature at McGill. From 1992-1994, I taught English in an Adult Basic Education program at Redstone Reserve in the Chilcotin territory. Since 1996, I have been developing and teaching the English program at the Institute of Indigenous Government located in Vancouver. During this period, I helped to publish an in-house literary magazine entitled <u>Drumbeats</u>. Currently I am working as a co-host for the IIG radio-show called Historical and Current Indigenous Perspectives on 102.7 FM–CRFO.

Suzanne Rancourt

Born and raised in West Central Maine, Suzanne Rancourt is Abenaki, Bear Clan, and is a USMC and Army Veteran. She is an internationally published writer, a mentor for Wordcraft Writers' Circle, a singer-songwriter who has performed nationally, and an independent education consultant. Suzanne holds a Master of Fine Arts in Poetry from Vermont College and a Master of Science degree in Educational Psychology from SUNY, Albany, NY. She is the Parent Education Specialist for a Head Start program in northern NY.

Janet Marie Rogers

Janet is of Mohawk/Tuscarora ancestry living in Victoria, BC. She has self-published her writings since 1997 to make a series of six chapbooks to date, under the name, Savage Publishing. Janet enjoys reading her works publicly and has incorporated movement and performance into her presentations.

Armand Garnet Ruffo

Armand Garnet Ruffo (Ojibway) is the author of a collection of poetry, Opening in the Sky (Theytus Books, 1994) and a poetic biography, Grey Owl: the Mystery of Archie Belaney (Coteau, 1997). A new collection of poetry, At Geronimo's Grave, will appear in the spring of 2001 from Coteau Books. His plays include an adaptation of his book on Grey Owl. Ruffo's poetry, stories and essays have appeared in numerous literary journals and anthologies including, Voices of the First Nations (McGraw-Hill Ryerson, 1996), Literary Pluralities (broadview, 1998), An Anthology of Canadian Native Literature in English (Oxford, 1998) Native North America (ECW, 1999), and An Introduction to Literature (Nelson, 2000).

Amy-Jo Setka

Amy-Jo Setka is Metis, a happy newlywed who has just completed two years at the En'owkin Centre and is enrolled at the SUNTEP program at University of Saskatchewan. I plan to learn my kohkum's language, Cree, and continue writing.

Kim Shuck

Kim Shuck is a basket artist and educator. She holds an MFA in textiles. Her baskets have been shown nationally around the United

States as well as internationally. Her educational publications include a piece in <u>Math and Science Across Cultures</u>, a book developed through the Exploratorium in San Francisco. Shuck grew up in a mixed race home. Her father is Tsalagi and her mother is Polish. She feels that she learned more about communication, patience and humour in that house than from anything her experiences at the University gave her. She is trying to pass those insights on to her three children.

Richard Van Camp

Richard Van Camp is a member of the Dogrib Nation. He is the author of a novel, <u>The Lesser Blessed</u>, and two children's books: <u>A Man Called Raven</u> and <u>What's The Most Beautiful Thing You Know About Horses?</u> illustrated by George Littlechild. His radio play "Mermaids" was narrated by Ben Cardinal and broadcast several times for CBC Radio's 1998 "Festival of Fiction."

Gerry William

I was born in Enderby, BC, and am a member of the Spallamcheen Indian Band. I graduated with a Bachelor of Arts Degree in English Literature in 1975 from the University of Victoria. I have spent my entire adult life working with, and for, First Nations communities. I have been a Native courtworker, a senior trainer, an executive director, a teacher and a counsellor. I have also been chair of several major First Nations organizations, from the B.C. Native Peoples Credit Union to the Allied Indian & Métis Society. Currently, I teach at the Nicola Valley Institute of Technology in Merritt, BC. I am nearing the completion of my Ph.D. Program in First Nations Studies from the Union Institute in Cincinnati, Ohio. I also chair the Education Council at NVIT, and am President of the NVIT Employees Association. I love writing and my latest novel (just completed) depicts the history of the North Okanagan at First Contact.

Vera M. Wabegijig

Vera M Wabegijig is Anishnaabe from Mississauga First Nation in Ontario. She is from the Bear Clan, twenty-six years old, mother,

ex-En'owkin student, and an ex-UVIC student who now lives in
Vancouver with her partner Larry and their daughter Storm and will
be expecting a new edition in a matter of weeks. Her poetry can be
found in previous <u>Gatherings</u>, <u>Our Words</u>, <u>Our Revolutions</u>, <u>My
Home as I Remember</u>, <u>Breaking the Surface</u>, and an essay in
<u>Reclaiming the Future: Women's Strategies for the 21st Century</u>.

Other Authors

Larry Nicholson
Dan Ennis
Rasunah Marsden